Love Finds Max Royster at Christmas

or

Kissing in the Slush After Sixty

LOVE FINDS MAX ROYSTER AT CHRISTMAS

OR

KISSING IN THE SLUSH AFTER SIXTY

A Max Royster Mystery

by Frank Hickey

Dedicated to
The Enchantress of My Life,
M.H.Z., from China.

CHAPTER 1

Dreaming
or
Does the World Fall in Love?

Cold weather turned me cranky but Sinatra's tape cheered me as he sang "The Christmas Waltz" and I saw a long-legged dark blonde woman under green Noel lights at the dance.

"The song says," I said to her. "Right now is when the whole world falls in love."

Nerves cracked my voice.

"Kind of like a traditional pickup line," she said. "From some loser."

"Tonight's the Holiday United Dance Festival, "I went on." So, how can we show unity unless we dance?"

"Dance like this?"

"Just like this," I said. We danced and spun around. A Black man, bumped into me, talking to himself. Others stepped away from him.

Snow and slush lay everywhere.

"Mayor's idea, this Unity Festival to bridge this frontier, here on Lexington Avenue and Ninety-Six street," I said. "The boundary between the elegant, snooty Upper East Side and the broken-bottle Spanish Harlem."

"That's changing," she said. "Spanish Harlem's going yuppie now. Upscale. Like everyone wants to be."

"Meaning you?" I asked.

"The restaurant where I work cut my hours to three days. Economy, my boss says. D'you think that I want to grow old and fat working as a part-time barmaid? Paying too much rent while smiling at jerks?"

We danced more. The Black man stumbled nearby.

"There's a good crowd here already," I said. "Set up the marketplace, selling everything. Scarves, souvenirs, hardware and jewelry. We New Yorkers WILL shop, even in this cold."

A young cop, blond hair under the uniform eight-point hat, bellied past us, equipment jangling in the frosted air. He frowned at the Black man. Now the Black man was staggering and waving his hands. The cop's chest swelled out against the dark blue winter-weight jacket.

Pouter-pigeon, I told myself, and a sour, dour fella.

The cop moved up on the Black man.

Cold lashed each inch of me and I missed California's desert heat. Framing a smile on my face, I tried speaking to her again.

"This may sound like another cliché –" I began.

"Again?"

"– but if you want to rise in Manhattan society, I can help," I finished.

Her tilted nose bobbed upwards near dark greenish eyes.

"RIGHT THERE, FELLA!" the cop shouted.

He pushed the same Black man sideways. The man grabbed him. They went against a garage wall.

"Halt!" the cop hollered.

They slopped against each other.

"Stay here," I told her.

"Bull," she snapped. She jerked free of my dance hold. I staggered back on my heels. She ran to the fight.

The cop and the Black man punched and kicked down the garage ramp. Darkness swallowed them. She followed. I could not see any of them.

"Are you mad?" I shouted.

BOP!

My training kicked in.

"Shots fired!" I shouted.

My body sprawled out of range.

The woman was already down the ramp. Her heels clattered.

"Stray slug, get you blown right into rock 'n' roll heaven," I grunted.

I lurched to my feet and down the ramp and grabbed her black coat by the sleeve. It smelled of patchouli incense.

Farther down the curved ramp, the cop held his gun on the Black man. The Black man lay still. Cordite edged the air.

"Get back!" I hissed at the woman. "Clear out of here!"

"But I saw what happened!" she shouted.

Her words echoed up the garage ramp. A crowd formed on the ramp.

"Hear that?" a round Latino man with a short beard said. "And the brother's dead!"

"He's not dead," I snapped. I hoped that was true.

"Get back, all of you!" the cop yelped. He waved the blocky black Glock gun at the crowd. "He tried for my gun!"

"That's what they all of them say!" the Latino man said. "While they killing our people!"

"You didn't see anything!" I whooped at my dance partner. "You couldn't. It was too dark."

"I did!" she said.

"Yo, they fixing things!" a stringy White kid on a skateboard whooped on the ramp. "He can't get away, covering up!"

Some started down the ramp.

My hand caught her arm and yanked her upwards, towards the street.

"Get your hands off me!" she cawed.

"Better me than them," I said.

"Who?"

"Get her!" someone shouted. "Both of them!"

Three bodies blocked me. Tucking my head, I bulled into them and burst onto the street. A sales table broke and splintered as I slammed into it. Trinkets and jewelry spattered onto the sidewalk.

She broke free of my grip. Her coat gaped open. Two others grabbed her, one between her legs, under the short skirt. Necklaces and monogrammed spoons crunched under my foot.

Panting, I looked for anything to hit or cut. My fingers found a pair of scissors in a tan suede case. I spun around. The suede case slipped off and bared the scissors.

"Let go of her!" I shouted. "Or I cut you!"

"I got her, Ace!" the Grabber said. "She's mine."

CHAPTER 2

Grabbin' and Stabbin'
or
Best That I Can

I lunged forward.

The scissors in my grip bit his wrist. Many nerves nestled there.

"YEEOW!" he hollered. "You cut me!"

"Pricked," I said. "Pricked you. Think it over."

Like always, trouble made me crack wise.

He grabbed his pricked wrist. The woman head-butted him without taking a breath. His nose spurted red. He rocked backwards.

"Don't get grabby," she said. "Not with me."

"No, ma'am," I said.

"Wasn't talking to you."

"I'll answer for him," I said. "He is now somewhat indisposed. I'm Max."

"Peg," she said.

The Grabber dropped.

"You broke my nose!" he whined.

"Don't say anything about the dead guy," I said to the woman, Peg.

"But I saw what happened!"

"Don't tell me. You want bomb threats where you work, subpoenas, jail for contempt, New York hating you for a liar, gotta move away? Believe me, it will happen. So, just hush up now. Don't move from here."

"Who are you, ordering me around?" she said.

She vexed me. But looking at her excited face thrilled me. It had been a long time now, being alone.

"Do something!" she cawed.

Her words pushed me back down the garage ramp. The cop sat near the body. The cop was crying, still holding the gun. He looked shocked, unable to register me or anything else.

Kneeling down, I frisked the dead man and scrutinized him. He lay about my weight, 220, and a burly five feet ten. A clownish, Black round face, missing some teeth, looked back at me. Ignoring my blues, I leaned closer and sniffed.

A sweetish candy odor came from the mouth with gappy teeth. There was no liquor or marijuana scent. His hair was cut short, almost military, and he was closely shaved. He looked about 68, a few years older than I. A heavy green field jacket covered a blue turtleneck sweater. His pants were thick blue jeans and my hands made sure that he had no weapon or knife anywhere.

A tan cell phone suffering a cracked screen, a black leather wallet with a few singles mushed together and house-keys on a leather fob were in his pockets.

The left wrist had a tattoo. Maybe it was a gang insignia. In the strong garage light, I saw the globe-and-anchor design, next to the words "Death before Dishonor----United States Marine Corps."

I trudged back up the ramp to the street, Peg and the crowd.

"What did she see?" a rangy pale White man with a shaved head and baby blue glasses said.

"We need to know."

"Get back!" I shouted.

"I will not," he said. "Who gave you power to order us?"

That stopped me.

He grabbed Peg. Peg twisted her wrist from his grip and broke free.

"You're no bodyguard, that's for sure, dude," she said. She made a face, with her pug nose against the brass-colored hair and darkish skin. Her black wool coat, trimmed with suede, gaped open. She whipped around, turning her back on me. Her legs caught my eye.

"Aren't you freezing in those black stockings?" I asked. "Though they look great on you."

"Customers like them," she said.

"But there's a tear, a run, in the left one," I said.

"Stop looking at my legs and get me out of here."

"I got a way," I said, looking at the scissors in my pocket.

Mother-of-pearl glistened in the center and filigree metalwork showed antique styling. Someone with craftsmanship had designed them. The blades were generous, about four inches long. Up close, it made a wicked, pretty weapon.

"He just executed that man!" a Latina teenager wearing a parka with a huge blond fur hood shouted. "That's how the po-po do us all the time!"

Blue-and-white NYPD cars sluiced down Lexington Avenue, cherry roof lights bleeding.

"CLEAR THAT SIDEWALK!" a woman cop's voice in a gruff city accent railed over the loudspeaker. "OR YOU ALL GOIN' JAIL, RIGHT NOW!"

"Always the light touch," I said. "Delicate and scholarly."

Jamming the scissors between my wide-banded wristwatch and my frozen left wrist, I tested snapping my arm down. The scissors slid into my left palm. It would work. Someone frisking you ignored the wrists.

"Good weapon, in close," I said to Peg.

"Get a damn gun."

"Hate guns."

"My bodyguard hates guns?"

"Yup."

"Scared of them?"

"Among many other things, yes."

"My hero," she said.

"'tis a consummation devoutly to be wished," I said. "Hold that thought. Be right back."

Cops crowded past. They streamed down the garage ramp. Their hands flicked at their Glock gun butts, like kids dandling a favorite bauble.

"Move it, people," the same woman cop's voice said. "This is a crime scene."

"Crime scene, yeah, all right," the same man with glasses who had seized Peg spat out. "You killed that man for no reason!"

CHAPTER 3

Law Leaps Out
or
Whistle Up the Irregulars

"The eternal argument," I said. "Hidden killers everywhere. Nobody trusts nobody."

"Hey, chief," a thin-faced woman cop with a throat tattoo of a pink pig said. "You gonna block things here, talkin' smack, or move on, like we told you?"

"Sorry, Officer," I said. "You're right. Talking too much philosophy."

"C'mon, Peg," I said. "Let's cross Lex, drift away."

"Let's go to that park over there. Why're you so bossy? Teach kindergarten or something?"

"Ballroom dance teacher. Just on commission, no salary –"

"– With your manners, you must starve. –"

"– was on the cops."

"And?"

"Some trouble."

"Pension?"

"Dream on," I said.

The park sprouted green on the southeast corner of Lexington and 96th, with a playground, swings and a slide, and a grey stone shed.

My cell phone felt cold against my fingers. Gazing at Peg in her suede-trimmed coat and slim legs in black stockings warmed me.

The first call was to Leo, the most jolly six-fingered super in Manhattan.

"GNA OY NAY," he lisped into the phone. Years ago, he had asked me how to say "I love you," in Cantonese. Once I had taught him the words 'GNA OY NAY,' his Puerto Rican soul had thrilled to the Cantonese cadence and he answered all of my phone calls with that phrase.

"Call the Irregulars," I said. "Lex and 96th. Somebody's dead."

Punching in Nancy's number, I blew out another breath into the chill. The scissors felt cold against my left wrist.

"Whozzis?" Nancy's Kansas drawl slurred into my ear.

"I'm your rescue demon. Max. Got a client right here and now to make you rich."

Wanna sleep."

"What you want is cash to bail out Santiago, your fancy-man, the next time that he gets cracked for drug sales."

"He's addicted to it."

"And you to him. You've still got your lawyer's ticket, right?"

"Haven't had client one in years, Max."

"Fall out in your jammies to Lex and 96th, and you've got one."

"You there?"

"I'll be the one lecturing the cops on how not to start a riot," I said. "Because there's one starting up right now. And, counselor, call out the Irregulars."

"Why try? Sixteen degrees outside."

"Money, counselor."

"Why aren't you with your beloved Koy?" she asked. "Snowy slush night like this."

It hurt me to speak.

"She left," I said. "Chinese culture clash. No security. She's much younger than I."

"Max, are you crying?"

"Kind of."

"I can tell."

"Nancy, if you don't briefcase on down here, some law-yer-shark will. And they won't give a good damn about truth, justice or what really happened tonight."

More sirens blocked our talk.

"No more Koy," she said.

"Can't talk —"

"You're hurting," she said. "Be right down."

Cop vans hit the corner. Clumps of cops, mostly White youngsters in black puffy jackets, spilled out onto the sidewalk.

"Those cops look and sound like a high-school team," I told Peg.

"Which they were, a few years ago."

More cars disgorged men.

"Here's more company, Peg," I said. "Lookit those dark raincoats with precious gold bits pinned to the lapels. Detectives, some lieutenants and an inspector. Captain Day, my old nemesis in this precinct, must be to home, sleeping in his jammies on this frosty night."

A pearl-gray sharkfin Cadillac, this year's model, shining like a jewel, lanced down Lexington Avenue and stopped near us.

A Black man, broad and solid, bounded out.

His baritone rolled across the avenue.

"You all seen me on TV," he said. "Skip Cossee. Call me 'Daddy Fix.' Best lawyer for the people. Who wants some MONEY?"

"Oh, no," I said. "Not again."

Peg stared at him.

Skip saw her. He homed in on her.

"Pretty lady, you want some money," Skip crooned. "And I bet you saw the whole murder."

"Why call it murder?" I asked.

Skip did not miss a beat.

"Maxwell, you friends with this pretty lady, you can tell her all about me —"

"You wouldn't want that," I said.

"— and how I help folks who need it. Suffering —"

"Cue the organ," I said.

"Wise guy?" the Cadillac driver said. He bulled out onto the sidewalk. He stood more than my six feet in height and much bigger across the chest. Pale freckles dotted his face as his jaws worked, scanning me.

The mouth hung open, like he did not care about me trying to hit him there. Boxers knew that punching an open jaw snaps the bone easily. Smart fighters clenched their mouths shut.

He looked like muscle.

His eyes had that glacial look of someone just following orders from the boss. He could gut me on a spit or break me down, ripping tendons. Fear fluttered my body valves.

"Never know the answer to that question," I said.

"Talk that way about Mr. Cossee, then you got a problem with me."

CHAPTER 4

Real Life
or
Max Meets Muscle

His lips skinned back over his teeth. This hulk reminded me of the bigger bullyboys of the Saint Blaise School for Young Men, where I had suffered as a schoolboy.

"Look at you," the Muscle said. "You nothing."

"Well," I said.

"Threatening us. Pal, I would love to bust into you."

My legs shook.

"Oh, no," I said, trying to mock him. But my voice shook. That ruined my routine. "That sounds like it would hurt,"

"Now, darling," Skip said to Peg, waving a thick hand at the end of his black leather coat sleeve. "You an' me, need some warming up and talking turkey, without interruptions, till we can get the straight story on what happened here tonight."

"Why should I do that?"

"My card here. Google me. See that everyone, the System, they all scared, this one fat Black man. Get me in front of a jury, and I tell 'em, story of Goliath and the lion."

"So?"

"Like the way you ask your questions –"

"Bottle it," I hissed.

"– nice and direct. Be a pleasure getting you that money. We can work real swingin', you an' me. Sue this trigger-happy cop. And his sergeant, lieutenant and Academy. All the way up the chain of command. Shake up that piggy bank that the city is holding onto."

"New York's fulla lawyers."

"True, very true. See many of them out here, this cold corner, ready to tote you 'way from all this mess?"

As if he heard Skip, across Lexington, my friend Leo drifted into the growing crowd. He wore a pink bobble-type wool cap. It was part of the silliness outfit that every New Yorker picked to get through the winter. Under it, he sported an enormous tweed overcoat, bulky pants and Army boots.

He was dressed to spend the night outdoors, if necessary. Even from where I was, his gold teeth gleamed as he grinned at some of the crowd

A hefty Black woman wearing an orange parka with a yellow rooster on the front laughed at something Leo said. Behind them, my other pals, Tisa and Ivan, chatted up more crowd members.

Nancy the lawyer had called them out on this frozen night. That made me smirk.

"See those suits across Lexington?" I asked Peg.

Skip's big head snapped up at my words.

"Those slices of cream dress shirts above their collars," I babbled on. "No overcoats. That means that they don't expect to be outdoors for a long time. They are bosses. That makes this death a big one."

"Too big for you!" Peg snapped.

"Not in this neighborhood," I said. "I call this Upper East Side 'The Playpen.' Because you can live and die here, around all this gentility and cash, without ever having to grow up. And I already have a team of trained investigators, my Playpen Irregulars, here now, talking up the crowd, schmoozing, flirting and finding those big talkers who saw everything. So you should throw in with me."

"Trained by who? FBI? NSA?"

"By me," I said.

"Oh, God."

"Actresses, barflies, characters, ballroom dancers, therapists, saloon singers, volunteers in the highest American tradition of Lexington and Concord."

"Maxwell," Skip said. He played at noticing me again. "Hey, baby, you going into competition agin' The Old Man?"

"How you doing, Skip?" I asked, playing for time.

"Oh, baby!" he rolled his actor's voice. "They doing it to me. I'm afraid to turn around. Might like what I see."

"You two KNOW each other?" Peg asked, in her breathy, little-girl voice.

"Too long," I said.

BAM!

Something exploded.

My head screamed.

WHAM!

The Muscle was hitting me.

Frozen sidewalk hit my face.

"Talking all kinda smack 'bout Mr. Cossee," the Muscle panted. "He's a LAWYER."

He kicked at my throat.

CHAPTER 5

Max Ducks
or
Leo Loves

Mother Royster taught me how to duck.

I ducked.

His foot caught my head, in the back. But I was already rolling. Something hard stopped me. A big car loomed above my head. The tire was blocking me.

To fake him, I got to my knee.

He kicked again. I dodged.

His foot hit the car.

"MUTHA!"

"Leave Mom out of this," I panted. "Thanks, Detroit."

I scooted under the big car.

The engine felt warmer than the air. Maybe some fat-cat detective boss had driven it here. The Muscle did not know what to do. He tried grabbing me under the car chassis.

"Come outta there!" he shouted.

"Why?" I asked. "I like it here."

Under the car smelled of cold asphalt, gas and dirt.

"You a punk!"

"Perhaps," I said. "But here feels tolerable. Better than what's waiting for me out there."

"Maxwell," Skip's voice boomed from behind me. "Always did talk too much."

Freezing, I pushed myself out onto the street. The Muscle was too stout to run. He could not catch me.

Something clobbered my jaw.

"Wrong again," I hissed.

Muscle could move.

Muscle threw another jab.

Terrified, I bobbed out of range.

"Where the good citizens?" I panted. "Raising the hue-and-cry against this thuggery?"

"Stop running away!" Peg shouted at me. "Stand up and fight him!"

The crowd across Lexington Avenue was growing larger.

Ivan, my Playpen Irregular friend, had corralled a woman dog-walker, laughing with him and pointing at the blue-and-white NYPD cars. The cars were now humping up on the sidewalks, like building blocks tossed by a spoiled kid. One cop, slim, young, looking like a marathon runner, was smacking his gloves together, trying to stay warm.

"Hey, hey!" I bellowed across Lexington. "Please! MOS needs help!"

That brought the cop's head up.

"Yo! Yo!" he shouted at his buddy cops.

He sprinted at me, like I knew he would. Long ago, I had been an active cop and I knew the signs.

The buddy cops whooped and shambled across Lexington towards me, gun belts and tools jangling. Bystanders joined them.

Watching a crime scene on a frozen night was boring.

Leo was with the bystanders. His gamin face split open to show a smile. His eyes zeroed in on mine as I hatched a scheme.

"SEAS ARRESTADO!" I sang out.

One cop, Latina, bulky in her coat, turned pink-framed glasses at me. Her lip red gloss shone in the streetlight, next to a lock of hair dyed blonde.

"Who you talking to, buddy?" she asked. "You said 'Get Arrested' in my lingo."

Leo saw his moment. He obeyed me.

"Hello, I love you, sweetie-pie!" Leo shouted at the Latina cop.

The first cop reached the spot near Muscle and me. His metal baton pointed at us both.

"You two knock it off!" he shouted.

"Be a pleasure," I said.

"We pals," Muscle said. "Just playing round. Sorry, Officer."

"Must be Skip trained you well," I said. "How To Duck Arrests 101."

"Love, love, love!" Leo whooped.

Moving fast, he darted at the Latina cop and grabbed her in a bear hug.

"Love-ah you, sweetie-pie!" he roared.

The cop flung him down onto the sidewalk.

"Don't bust my chops!" she shouted at Leo.

"Lock him up, Francesca!" one cop with a handlebar moustache turning white said. "Can't did you like that."

From the asphalt, Leo reached up to grab her left ankle and kiss it.

"We gonna be real happy, MAMITA!" he crowed.

"Okay, hump!" the Latina cop shouted. "You're in!"

The Latina cop swooped down, forced Leo's hands together and cuffed them. Carefully, I avoided the cop's baton and Muscle, talking to Peg.

"I know where I saw you before, Peg," I said. " Subway Inn."

"Subway Inn? No way. That train wreck? Try Sessions 73 cafe. Work there."

"I got confused. Know your spot. Good food."

Now, I knew where Peg worked.

"Peg, we don't need to talk much to Max now," Skip said. "Just you go along with Joey."

The Sprinter cop edged closer. His nickel nameplate read "Dahl."

"You guys just hacking around?" Dahl asked. "Is that it?"

"Absolutely, Officer," the Muscle, the bruiser that Skip had called Joey, said. His chest still heaved and his eyes burned to hurt me but his voice stayed cool.

Behind them, the Latina cop was standing the laughing Leo up to his feet.

"You're busted for Assault on a Police Officer," she said, "and Obstruction of Governmental Administration."

"All that for hugging," I wisecracked.

"You're in a big jam now, fella," the Latina cop said to Leo. "Putting you through the system. Guys in Central Booking like, getcha, show you love, dude."

"Maybe teach you a new way," I said.

Leo blew kisses at the cop.

"Let's go," Peg said. "I'm with you, Skip. Not this loser Max. I like my men strong."

CHAPTER 6

Talking Shop
or
New Threats

Peg's words pushed me back a step.

"Rather blunt lady," I said.

Joey opened the passenger door of Skip's Cadillac, seated her and drove away.

"That stings," I said under my breath.

Her words cut deeper than I could gauge. Tomorrow, I might think about them. Maybe. I wanted her. It had been too long alone.

"Wassup, Maxwell?" Skip boomed. Under the streetlight, he picked his way closer to me. He had aged a bit since our last talk and seemed fuller in his face with high cheekbones and eloquent brown eyes. He stood about five seven and looked to weigh a solid two hundred and forty pounds, with wide shoulders and no fat jiggling anywhere that I could ever see.

"You getting bigger," I said.

"And badder," he answered.

"In a film, they might cast you to play the role of the village blacksmith. Big enough. That rolling walk you got. From that derringer gun in your ankle holster."

"What's that?" the cop named Dahl asked. "You carrying, bro'?"

"Duly licensed with a full, unrestricted carry permit," Skip sang out sweetly. "Both available for inspection at any time."

"Like now?" he asked.

"If you have reasonable suspicion, as the courts define it, yes. Keeping in mind that without you seeing a bulge or information supplied to you by a source known to have been truthful to you in the past, you have no right to harass a hardworking Black defense lawyer just because he's at the scene of one of your fatal screw-ups where another Black man lies dead —"

"Excuse me," Dahl said. "Got something else here to handle."

Behind Dahl's back, Skip hiked up his pants leg to show his derringer in a suede-and-sheepskin ankle holster, grinning like a street kid. The gun gleamed in the streetlights.

Dahl turned to face me.

"When you were messing with that guy," Dahl said. "You shouted out 'MOS needs help.' Us cops, pal, those words 'MOS' means 'Member Of the Service.' Other words, cop. That's why I jumped in. Don't like civilians phonying themselves off as cops. Get me, pal?"

"Yup," I said. "But I used to be on The Job."

He put out a wiry hand.

"Give," he rasped.

Making one of my strangest and ugliest faces, I gave.

"Got some paper here," he mused.

"It's a paper world," I said.

"Huh?"

"So I hear."

"Paperwork's all funky, man. Do ya blow your nose on it or something? Here I can read where PO Maxwell A. Royster loses three vacation days for working two hours overtime without supervisorial authorization."

"'Supervisorial authorization,'" I said. "Just hearken unto dem woids, willya?"

"So, now you're retired, living big off your pension and messing with us real MOS?"

"No pension, Officer."

"What happened?"

"Absolutely nothing to get excited about."

"Ya need that pension, cuz," the cop said.

"I opine that you are correct," I said.

"Max?" Nancy's drawl came across the concrete behind me. She breathed heavy, eyes burning and her breasts heaving under a long loose coat, silk blouse, tailored jeans and high suede boots.

"You look striking, as always," I said. "Next to Peg –"

"Who's Peg?"

"Your client."

"Where's Peg?"

"In my mind's eye."

"Excuse me?"

"Everywhere and nowhere," I said. "Haunting the edge of my eye."

Nancy tossed me a look that looped back into the past.

"Max, again?"

"Christmas," I said.

"Better not," she said.

"Can't."

Dahl the cop gazed at Nancy. His eyes warmed. The radio on his hip cackled.

"All you guys, get to the command center," a wet and chewy city accent said over Dahl's radio. "Crowd here growing, getting more disorderly."

"Later, cuz," Dahl said to me. "Here's your garbage back."

His long fingers crisped my NYPD papers back to me.

"My RE-SOOM," I said. "Or resume. Future passport to glory."

Three characters shambled up from the park at 95th Street, bellowing at each other. They sported lightweight clothes. That meant that they were too drunk to feel the cold.

They looked about 22, the years when loud talk and liquor ruled them.

"My phone says some spade got iced here," the loudest one said. "Let's go look. Maybe kick some Black butt."

"Righteous, bro'," his buddy said.

One saw Nancy and pointed at her.

"Hey, lookit Lady jugs here!" he cawed. "Let's do her up!"

"Cops, dude!"

"Aw, they busy, man. Gotta park right here. Romantic."

My throat dried. They circled Nancy and me. Helicopters buzzed overhead.

"PO-LICE!" I shouted.

The helicopter noise covered my shout.

They moved in closer. One snapped out a switchblade knife and slashed the air.

CHAPTER 7

Woofin' and Knifin'
or
Plain Talk

The knifer moved in closer to me.

Nerves made me skitter backwards. A garbage can behind me stopped my steps. I reached inside it to throw garbage at him. He came closer. My fingers found an empty Styrofoam meat holder. An idea hit me. It better work.

Nancy glided to the knife's left, pivoted and kicked at his knee. He slashed at her.

"Gottcha, crotch!" he snorted.

His buddies moved in. I hunched over, gripping the holder in both hands.

Her kick was a feint. He slashed and missed. He went off balance. She switched legs. Her left foot smashed into his ankle. He buckled.

"Owww!" he wailed. "That hurts!"

She kicked again, right shin, left shin and the right thigh. He dropped. She kicked the knife clear of his hand. It pinwheeled in the streetlight.

My hands snapped the holder in two. BAM!

It sounded like a shot.

Both his buddies jumped.

"Ya want the next shot?" I shouted. "Right inna head!"

They bolted.

"Language that they can comprehend," I said.

They kept running uptown, into Spanish Harlem.

Across Lexington Avenue, the cops kept milling around the growing crowd. A slim Black woman, on our side of Lexington, walked towards us. Something about her tugged at my memory.

"Not good chaps," I said. "Not gentlemen."

"Know that you never carry," Nancy said. "But that was a gunshot. Where you holding your gun?"

"Right here," I said. She gaped at the broken Styrofoam holder in my mitts. "Found this out when I worked Shoprite as a kid. Break a steak container, sounds like a firecracker. Or a piece."

"And they RAN?"

"They're bullies. They know that THEY would use a gun. So, they figure that I would. Plus, they're liquored up on giggle water. Not thinking well. If I say 'shot,' they think the same thing. Power of suggestion."

"Maybe you spent too much time in Hollywood."

"Does sound like California hot-tub philosophy, doesn't it?"

My hands reached down to the knifer. He rolled on the ground, gripping his knee.

"Nancy, d'you know that woman over by the corner?" I asked. "Seen her somewhere."

"Can't place her, huh? You're at the right age for dementia to really take hold."

"Thanks."

My hands frisked the knife-man, still moaning on the ground.

"Flashback from the Patrol years," I said. "Always check the hats."

I stripped the watch cap off his head. It smelled oily. A single-edge razor blade fell from the cap. He had been carrying the blade inside the cap's folded-up brim.

"Wo-how!" I said. "This blade could cut off my head. I once saw a goodly wife use that same blade to achieve widowhood in a rapid manner."

"I'm hurt," he said.

"Living nervous there, hero?" I asked. "Starting your own Department of Homeland Security?"

"Doctor –"

"Only if you tripped on the curb. Otherwise, we got cops, cops and more cops. And you go down for trying to cut her and me. So, curb. Okay?"

"You know what I'd like to do to that bitch?"

"Depends on where she bit you," Nancy said. Her cobalt eyes heated and glowed behind her glasses. Her smile sharpened.

"Leave him here," I said. "I'll have the cops call an ambulance."

We moved away from him. The Black woman came closer. She crouched and pointed a black gun at us.

"FBI!" she shouted. "Move and I shoot!"

CHAPTER 8

Reality
or
Just Like TV

I froze.

"Whenever someone shouts 'Freeze!' at me, I freeze," I whispered.

Nothing moved on my outside. Not a digit wavered.

From my eye's edge, I saw Skip step back and cross 95th Street. The crowd was growing larger there. Some gaped at this gunplay. Overhead, helicopters broke the chill ice night.

The Black woman gripped the gun two handed, pointing at us both. Her left hand held a folder with a gold badge bobbing on it. Both hands looked steady as a moon-rock on an astronaut's night-table.

"FBI!" the Black woman hollered. "Drop your gun!"

The cops across Lexington paid attention. Their hands hitched near their holsters.

"Hey, FBI!" Dahl shouted. "He got no gun!"

My hands opened. I was still holding the two broken pieces of Styrofoam from the meat container. The pieces dropped to the sidewalk. The Black woman squinted at them.

"I said 'Drop the gun!'" she shouted. "Not your trash!"

"No gun! Like the cops say!"

"We have no guns," Nancy said. "I'm his lawyer."

"Lawyer, shmoyer," Dahl said, coming closer. "Looks more like his main squeeze."

"Hey, FBI!" another cop hollered in a Caribbean accent hitching up his Sam Browne gun belt and shaking his crew cut Asian head. "Stand down, sweetheart. Let the real police deal with him."

"I take it that you're not calling me 'sweetheart,'" I said.

"Not ruddy likely," the same cop gave back.

"I heard a shot!" the woman said. "Put your hands up. I'm going to search you."

"When cats bark," I said.

"Excuse me?"

"You can't search me," I said. "Case you didn't notice, we are opposite genders. Rules prohibit you from frisking me. Unless it's an emergency. Which this ain't."

"If you move," the woman said, "I'll use necessary force against you."

"Leave him alone," Nancy said. "This is unwarranted Government harassment."

"Stand still," the woman said.

Blading her body the right way, in case I was trying to kill her, she moved up and frisked me. Her hands felt cold and hard, against my private parts.

Tonight, I was sporting my brown leather bomber jacket with the sheepskin lining and collar, black nylon windbreaker, blue denim work shirt and black no-name jeans, with my rubber-soled Patrol shoes. It felt like I was layering on fabrics to keep out the cold. Nothing looked elegant but it was not supposed to.

"Hey, FBI!" Dahl shouted. "Can't search him!"

"That's a civil rights violation!" another cop bellowed from a doorway, shadows hiding his face. "Why don't someone call the FBI? They handle civil rights violations, don't they?"

"Sure they do," Dahl said. "They do it by busting us cops."

"It's the only way to protect civil rights," the cop in the doorway said.

"Sometimes," I said.

"Let's put the FBI where the FBI puts us," the doorway cop said.

"Sounds like justice to me," I said. "Since we're talking philosophy here."

"Maybe we should arrest this nice FBI lady for assaulting Senior here," Dahl said. "Penal Law says that any unwanted physical contact is an assault."

"Go ahead and keep calling me 'senior,'" I said. "It really sends me."

Throwing a look over my shoulder at the woman and her gun, I recognized her.

"Special Agent Evers," I said. "I always knew that you would come back, hand-gunning your way into my life again."

CHAPTER 9

Old Friends
or
Catching Up

"Who, you?" she asked.

"Special Agent Evers, you wound my feelings," I said. My hands stayed up. "Remember the Van Leer kidnapping just before Christmas, here in this oh-so-tony rich neighborhood?"

She blinked. Her dark face twisted behind gold-rimmed granny glasses.

"So, what?" she said. "What that got to do with the price of cotton in Bogalusa?"

"You remember me now?"

"I remember that you a hot mess. A soup sandwich, trying to play cop."

"But you see that I had no gun with me."

"You shot SOMETHING. The Bureau tested me, just as it tests all agents, in hearing and our Gunshot Recognition and Appreciation course at Quantico."

"You FBI types love naming courses, don't you?" I asked. "Have a name for everything. Pray tell, how do you 'appreciate' a gunshot?"

"You stalling, man. With you big words. Where the gun?"

"What happened to the precise diction, Special Agent?" I asked.

"Gun."

"That'll do, Special Agent," I said. "That's enough capricious and peremptory frisking, even from an opponent like you. There's nothing connecting me to any crime."

"Dunno, pal," Dahl said. "We all heard something, sounded like a shot."

"'Right, you," Evers said. "I'm from Missouri. That means 'Show me.' Missouri's state saying is 'Show Me.'"

"Proud, aren't you?" I asked, keeping my voice low.

"I'm not wrong," Evers said. "Know what I heard."

"As I just said."

"Go ahead, Max," Nancy said. "Show these guys what you do."

"Maybe you can appreciate this gunshot," I said. "Move back and holster up, Special Agent. Gather round, all you flatfeet. Might be something useful for you to learn. Maybe you'll stay cool the next time that you hear a biggish bang."

Bending down, still feeling the cold, I picked up the two broken pieces of the Styrofoam meat case.

"Got to use the larger bit here," I said. "Might not work so well. My hands, my meat-hooks, are not so very strong as you power-lifters are. But, we must try."

My whole frame gritted and tightened, holding the Styrofoam.

BAP!

It snapped.

Everyone flinched.

"Sounds just like a 25 cal or a 9 short," Dahl said. "'Frickin' amazing."

"Tricky guy," Evers said. "So tricky, might get yourself shot some day."

"For a guy who is not married, I can be very tricky," I said.

"You're making that noise," Dahl said. "That's a collar right there."

"For what?" I asked.

"Dis cond. Disorderly conduct. Or, like the young cops say 'disco'."

"Dahl, you look about twenty-four yourself, " I said. "How much younger could they be?"

"I'm gonna sue you losers," the Knifer said from the ground.

"Every last one of you."

"For what?" I asked. "Not letting you knife me?"

"Or me?" Nancy asked.

"If I wasn't busy, I'd take your lawsuit case," Skip said.

"We know," I said.

Dropping the Styrofoam bits into a garbage can, I walked over to the Knife-man and leaned down close to him.

"You talk about lawsuits and I will tell those cops to book you for Attempt Murder," I said. "And they'll crack you for it, just to get that arrest overtime. Tonight Saturday, no judges to see you until Monday. On the seventh day, the Lord of Justice rests. That means –"

"Why you talk so much, man?"

"My DNA. Tuesday, you get your prelim. Meanwhile, you sharing everything, including intimate living arrangements with gentlemen with whom you may clash politically on several topics –"

"Jeez, enough, huh? Give it a rest."

He pushed himself up off the chilled concrete and limped to a car and supported himself, breathing hard and kept moving down 96th Street.

"That's enough," Dahl said. "Everyone move off –"

"Why?" Nancy said. "I'm here to represent –"

"Nobody but yourself," Skip said. "You don't even got yourself no client yet. Stop chasing ambulances, counselor."

"I've seen you pimping TV newscasts for anything that pushes your own agenda," Nancy spat out. "So, don't lecture me about ethics!"

"Whoo, boy!" Dahl said. "Lawyer cat-fight."

"Hey, I luvya, too!" Leo shouted from inside a clutch of bluecoats.

"He's still here?" Dahl shouted. "Don't you guys know enough to process a collar fast and bring him to the precinct? Why not? Jeez, with all the bosses around here and what-not?"

"Love!" Leo repeated.

He fixed on Nancy's body in the open coat she wore.

"Nancy, button up fast," I said. "Leo just target-locked on you."

"Why, Mr. Royster" she asked. "After Kansas formwork, I'm damn sure never cold."

Still handcuffed, Leo broke loose from the cops.

"Hold it, chum!" Dahl shouted.

Leo lunged at Nancy. He knelt before her. He rapped his head against the sidewalk.

"Love, love, love!" he chanted.

"Me need it, you too need it, we all need it!"

CHAPTER 10

Insults
or
Fist Fighting

Skip's sharkfin Cadillac slewed around the corner on 96th Street and jerked to a stop. Sponge toy dice hanging from the rear view mirror danced, pink and jolly.

"I see Peg in there," I said without thinking.

"Sometimes, you're like an addict," Nancy murmured.

"Says which?" I asked.

"Doesn't matter WHAT I say," she said. "Addict."

Like a kid, I sprang towards the Cadillac.

Joey held the door open for Peg as she got out, black stockings showing under the suede coat.

"Move back on the sidewalk!" a cop shouted at the growing crowd.

"What you doing here?" Skip roared. "Supposed to put her in the hotel."

"Boss, I did," Joey said. "Got her settled. Croydon House. Then the desk called, said they'd screwed up and the room was going to someone else, big-shot from Africa somewhere, with media and bodyguards. Didja want me make a big stink there? Everyone knows you, that hotel."

"Take her to another one, fool!"

"Would, boss. But, thing is, you didn't get around to paying us this week –"

"Don't you save your mammy-jamming money?"

"But you couldn't pay us off this month –"

"Cause no money came in to ME!" Skip bellowed. "I SHOT the postman! He lying up there on the office floor, bleeding like a 'ho on Sunday."

"Gimme a good leaving alone," Peg said to me. Her voice lisped and whispered, holding her city accent.

That cut me again.

Her black right stocking showed a run, the same jagged tear as before. But it was on a different leg now. She had taken the stockings off and put them back on again.

Some blood dappled the stocking now.

"What's that?" I blurted out.

My body crisped with heat, through the cold.

"What's what?" she asked.

"That blood."

"Oh, Jesus. You think you own me? What's your problem?"

"YOU!"

"What?"

"I mean –" I groped. "What are you doing? With this ape?"

"Depends on what we do, I might bleed. Or maybe it's his blood. Huh?"

"That's enough of this Who-Shot Willie!" Skip bellowed.

"Don't want us talking?" I asked.

Inside, I felt shaky, like someone coming apart. Skip moved his bulk between us. His big Black hand fanned out cactus-colored green cash to Joey.

"Here's five. Put her somewhere clean."

"No," I said.

"Then, pick me up," Skip said.

"Don't ignore me, Skip," I said. "That's your genius, ignoring anything that doesn't help you. But I ain't letting you spirit her into your cash factory you call a law office."

The cops were too far away to hear but Joey heard. His face still twisted from Skip slamming him.

"Why you spying on her?" Joey shouted at me. "You tryinna get a squirrel shot?"

"A WHAT?" I asked.

"A sneaky peek at her hair pie."

"Charming," Nancy said. She came behind me. "Like all
sexists."

"Stand down, Maxwell," Skip said. "Don't want you getting hurt."

"I'll hurt YOU," I said, like a kid.

"Don't be silly," Skip said. "Joey, get moving."

My body slipped into a boxing stance, facing Joey chin
tucked, hands high and knees bent.

"Come on, Joey," I gritted.

Angry fought with scared in me. Everyone focused on me.

"You a old dude," Joey said. "Ain't squaring off, against
no oldster like you. Catch you a heart attack, something."

"Scared?" I asked, through clenched teeth.

I sure was. I was scared of losing Peg. And, I needed to
keep the words short now or else fear would crack my own voice.

Joey moved up closer to me. Boxer-style, I stepped back
at an angle.

He kept coming.

CHAPTER 11

Joey Shows Mercy
or
Old Timer's Day

Joey jabbed. Nerves made me weave underneath it.

He stepped closer.

He stopped.

"This is janky, man," he said. "Take off, pops. Shouldn't ya be home, playin' with your grand-kids?"

"How droll," I said. "Very droll."

Joey dropped his hands like a boxer daring me to attack and stepped back.

"Now, Joey," Skip sighed. "You know, Lord don't love ugly. No reason for you playing bo-dacious with Maxwell. Just take the young lady to our secondary hotel."

"NO!" I put out. "That's just what I don't want."

"Talking like a baby here, Maxwell. Who cares a flyer what YOU want?"

"Me. I do."

"Everyday ain't Christmas, Maxwell."

"Has she paid you anything yet?" I asked. "Even a dollar? Signed a contract? Then, how is she your client?"

"Cause she expressed a big mammy-jammin' desire to be my client. And that's all that it takes, in this state. Don't try playing lawyer here. I'm New York's swinging-est lawyer and what I say goes."

"Not tonight," I said.

Skip pulled his great staring eyes at me.

"What all this, Maxwell?" he said, too low for anyone to hear. "This ain't like you."

Whipping my hands sideways, to warm them, I squinted at the crowd across Lexington Avenue again.

"We are the Society To Stop Aggressive Police!" one pale White String Bean of a guy shouted. "That's S-A-P! SAP is our name and we will sap the strength of the White power structure"

"We stand against the evil police!" a Black woman in a puffy green windbreaker with peace symbols in chalk-white on it, chorused with him. "All New Yorkers should join us!"

"Maybe they will," I muttered.

More cops pushed words and moves against the crowd.

"Hey, there, goof-ball!" one Black cop shouted at the String Bean kid. "Whyn't you go down to Bellevue Psych Ward and see if your parts came in?"

"You work for me, Officer," the String Bean said. "So you can't talk to us that way. We are SAP."

"You can say that again," I said.

"And if you abuse your authority here in any way, you will be punished for it."

The Playpen Irregular, Ivan, moved through the crowd behind String Bean.

Ivan smiled in his chunky moon face under curly hair and painful-looking eyeglasses. He knew how to work this crowd. With his manner, Ivan could pick up every last bit of gossip dirt, sift it for value and refine it into detective's gold.

"This was supposed to be a Unity dance!" String Bean griped.

"Bringing together the Upper East Side, one of the world's richest neighborhoods, with one of the poorest, EL BARRIO, of Spanish Harlem. To start friendships. And what happens?"

"You tell me," I said.

"Another White cop just HAS to murder another Black victim. Totally unarmed, people."

"You got something to say?" the cop grated. "Write to THE TIMES. Or the ACLU. The American Communist Lawyers Union."

"That cop sounds kind of passé," I said. "Do cops still snarl about the Commies?"

"If you're my lawyer," Peg said to Skip, "get me out of here. Now. Or maybe you don't need me."

"Officers!" Skip bellowed above the crowd noise. "My client —"

"No, no cops," Peg hissed at him. "I'll handle him."

She stepped towards me, in her black boots, swaying side-to-side a bit.

"That's your own style of walking," I said to her. "Sideways. Important if I ever had to tail you on foot. Everyone walks differently. Tailing someone, you gotta know their gait."

"Planning to stalk me?" she asked.

Her darkish face showed under the heavy blonde hair with a parted rosebud mouth.

"Don't worry about Joey and me," she whispered. "He's just for now. But smart guys, bright talkers, they really turn me on."

"Nice to hear," I said. "I'll tell the next one I see."

"Silly. I mean you. You get me wet."

"And if I let you go now, next week, we'll be flying down to Rio?"

"Maybe we will. I'll make up my mind. You have a card? Give it to me. I'll call you."

"When a horse grows horns."

"No, I mean it," she said, leaning closer. Her perfume rose from her secret skin. "Where's your wallet, huh? Here? Or here?"

"Exciting me."

"Mmm. That's just the beginning. Only the beginning. Gimme that card. Now, I want it."

"Too cold for this," I said.

"Right. Car's nice and warm."

"Sure that you and Joey warmed it up nicely."

"Come on. Inside, I can search you better. Lemme show you."

Now we were inside Skip's warm sharkfin Cadillac.

"Nice jeans," she said. "Let my fingers do the work. Here, I got the wallet."

"Don't do that!"

"Why not?"

She took the card. Joey and Skip got in the front seat.

Exiting the car, I felt my body shaking from her touch.

"Don't spoil it," Peg said. "Leave now. I'll call you."

CHAPTER 12

Reality Hits
or
The Irregulars Mutiny

Joey zoomed Skip's Cadillac away, with Peg inside.

My Irregular, Ivan, drew near me.

"Hate the frigging cold," Ivan said. "Just like you. Blowing my nose everywhere, freezing, tryinna glad-hand these mooks here for tall tales and see you goofing off here."

At his words, my nerves twanged inside me.

"Wasn't goofing off, Ivan," I said.

"Like hell. Saw you. Get me and Tisa, warm bed, heating each other for this bullcrap, another White cop panicking, shooting a brother."

Ivan's eyes bulged and watered behind the black-rimmed union-plan glasses. "See this, I get all emotional. Big stuff. No wonder I got three wives and ain't hit thirty years old yet. Mess is what I am. Me and Tisa, we need our sleep. Working tomorrow. Want us to come out here, play caped crusader in the cold?"

"I gotta teach six dance classes tomorrow, Ivan. This death means more."

"You got us lumped up in this Boy Scout do-gooder group," Ivan said. "Fighting evil and vice here in the Upper

East Side. 'The Playpen,' as you call it. So, we're your Playpen Irregulars, working and risking our TUSHES for no money –"

"Know that's difficult in these post-Recession times –" I said.

"Not difficult. Impossible! Keep drumming into our gourds that the first field interview is vital at a crime scene."

"It is, Ivan," I said. Ignoring my own body screaming alarms, I tried slowing my speech down, hoping that he might mirror me that way. Using his name should help.

"Tell me again, prof."

"Because that's when helpers are most passionate and clear-headed about what they saw. No time to think it over, fret about retaliation. Or testifying. I preached all this to you Irregulars before. Nothing new."

"Then why waste time messing with that blonde that I saw you with?"

"Can't explain it."

"Guess not."

"Ivan, we're both freezing out here. Look, the cabbies are already picking up some of these hollering crowdsters."

"What's a 'crowdster'?"

"Come on, Ivan. You know what a 'gangster' is, I hope."

"Someone who belongs in a gang?"

"You are right," I said. That phrase 'You are right,' came out of the salesman's arsenal of word-weapons. That was all that anyone wanted to hear, anyway.

"So, Ivan, now you know what a crowdster is."

"Word games in the snow," Ivan said. "Stop being a kid just once, Max."

"You mean, grow up before dementia sets in," I said. "Might be too late already."

"I'm taking Tisa home before we die of cold," Ivan said. "And your boy-ass games. Drop me off your Irregulars list."

That froze me more.

"Ivan –"

"Shove it," he said. "Lemme alone, alright?"

He took Tisa with him, stalking mad away.

"We know what happened here tonight!" String Bean said. "Just the same as Ferguson, Staten Island or North Charleston.

A White cop killed an unarmed Black man and then weaves together a lethal fairy tale to hide his racist moves."

"We got art!" a woman alongside him shouted in a harsh New England accent. Her dark hair splayed out from under the white canvas and wool coat that she wore. She clenched her left fist and raised it above her head.

"Not now," Stringbean said to her. "When it does more good."

"Clenched fist salute," I said to Nancy, now moving up near me. "Haven't seen that salute in years and years. Goes back to the peace movement of the 1960s."

"Goes back farther than that," Nancy said. "International Communist salute from the Depression years. See old photos of Communists in the Spanish Civil War, 1936, throwing out that salute."

"I didn't know that. Don't know a whole truckload about radicals. But they sound like they know something about what went down tonight."

"You're wasting your time with them, Max. Getting out of this gol-danged Northerwind, phone some sleazy lawyers who never sleep. What do you know 'bout radicals, anyway? Just from movies, damn betcha?"

"Sometimes they fascinate," I said. "Sometimes they kill innocents, claiming that there are no innocents in their struggle."

"You're simplifying, Max. You have a lot to learn."

That cut me some more. Maybe I belonged out of this frost and in a friendly warm bed myself.

"Go phone your sleazies," I said.

Tensing my thigh muscles like I often do when nerves tingle, I limped near String Bean.

"Excuse me, sir," I said. "Your group interests me. What are you into?"

String Bean whipped his head around.

"What kind of question is that?" he shouted loud enough for the TV news cameras to hear with their electronics. "Are you some type of cop or something?"

CHAPTER 13

The Elite
or
We Mad Rads

"He can't be any type of officer," the dark haired woman said in her accent. What I had thought was a New England accent was actually an East Indian accent.

Max Royster, master detective. Maybe my ears were cracking up from the cold.

Now that I came closer in the street light, I could see that she was South Asian, from India, Pakistan or someplace nearby.

"I mean, really, that white hair and those wrinkles —"

"— character lines," I said.

"— can't think that they are recruiting geriatrics to serve as government spies, now, can we? Not about Krio, anyway."

"How right you are," I said, winging it. "Krio, that is."

"You knew him, did you?" she asked.

That settled it. She was talking up the dead man.

"Live in the neighborhood," I said. "If you call it living. Never knew his last name."

"Yates. Krio Yates."

"Oja, can't you keep quiet about this?" String Bean said. "I mean, for five minutes? Jesus H. Christ on little rubber crutches."

"But aren't you going to put up posters now?" I asked, to throw them off balance. "With his name on the posters? So everyone will know soon anyway?"

"Will we?" String Bean asked. "How do you know that?"

"It stands to reason. You can't seek justice through publicity for a death and not name the dead victim. It wouldn't be much of a movement, right?"

"You seem to know a lot about this," String Bean said. "Radical actions, I mean, like."

Today too many speakers overused the word 'like'. Another reason to spurn String Bean.

"I lived through the Sixties," I said.

"Well, we've moved on since then," String Bean said. He wore a complex moustache and brief beard combination of sandy tufts. The beard and moustache dominated his narrow face.

His blue eyes darted over me, with manic twitches. Red rims showed around the eyes. He did not look healthy, especially in this cold. He looked like he would cough and sneeze a lot through winter, hacking up phlegm, thin and almost tubercular. He reminded me of sketches of Edgar Allen Poe, with the same piercing direct glare.

String Bean moved his body like someone who had never exercised. Maybe he believed in the Life of the Mind.

If he moved fast, those elongated bones would rattle and clack. Right now, I was going to try to rattle and clack them myself.

"Doesn't SAP want all types of persons in it?" I asked.

"The ones we trust, yes," String Bean said.

"My name's Max," I said, stretching out a palm like a Hail-Fellow-Well-Met at a Rotarian luncheon.

"I don't shake hands," String Bean said.

"Really? Must be something political."

"We don't need comedians in SAP," he said.

"Don't be too sure."

"I'm Oja," the South Asian woman said in her sing-song accent. It sounded sweet to my ears. "Why do you want to join SAP tonight? Isn't this rather sudden?"

"Thought about these cops a lot," I said. That was no lie. "And seems like, they're getting worse. Stop-and-frisk stuff, jacking people up for no reason, back-shooting them. Where is all this leading to?"

"Police state," Oja said. Her dark brows knitted prettily. "What kind of society do we have, that lets policemen abuse anyone they single out?"

It was time to get off police brutality and milk some more about Krio Yates.

"Sometimes I saw that Krio had some problems," I said. "Diabetes. He suffered that all the time."

"You really knew him well," Oja said.

"They thought he was drunk," String Bean said, "but diabetes without enough insulin, disoriented him."

"Can that happen?" I asked. "You know more about diabetes than I do."

Oja bobbed her head. Like many South Asian women, the food groups available had kept her petite. She only came up to my coat collar. Her eyes sparkled with wit, looking me over. She smirked at my careless clothes and hair.

"Perhaps the cop thought that Krio was drunk and therefore more dangerous," I said, testing them.

"Does that matter?" String Bean said. "I hear how cops talk to Black people. They cheapen them. This is one case that they can't cover up."

"You are right," I repeated. "That's why I want to join."

"No way, dude."

"Oh, come on, Justin," Oja said. "He looks all right. Sign him up."

"No!"

"Do it for me?" she said.

AHA! I thought. There was love among the revolutionaries. Or something like love.

"Hear me out," I said, lying again. "My lover just left me, after three years. Don't unhappy lovers make good radicals?"

"Huh?" he asked.

"That's what I always heard," I said.

"From who?" he asked.

"You mean 'whom', don't you?" I said. "Can't recall."

"We only take new members on recommendations."

"Not real radical. Are you running a political strike force or an apartment co-op board?"

CHAPTER 14

Confusion
or
Revolutionary Fondling

"Why can't he join?" Oja trilled in her accent. "He looks a robust chap —"

"Thank you," I said.

"— If somewhat old."

"Thanks just withdrawn," I said. "That kind of talk rips deeper each year."

"The powers that be want us smashed," String Bean said. "They own corporations, politicians and the media. And they still want to smash the voice of conscience, such as we."

"Justin, everybody knows this."

"No, they don't," I said. "Too many forget our struggle for human rights. Let me break up this revolutionary chit-chat by saying that you are wrong, young lady —"

"Don't patronize me with that sort of dialectic," Oja said.

"Sorry. What does your name 'Oja' mean?"

"In one of our hill languages in India, it means 'without impurity.'"

"Or maybe 'not without impurity?'" I said.

"Do not make me blush. I see that you fancy yourself some type of rogue."

"Only with words."

"And you talk too much," String Bean said. "We don't need that in SAP. So, stop bothering us. We are serious committed individuals and we have important work to do."

"My Lord, listen to yourself," I said. "How pompous. We are sounding like our own parents, their generation. We swore that could never happen."

"Let us delay this fascinating discussion until another time," Oja said. "Being small, I feel the cold more than you two. May we postpone?"

"But I need to get married," I said. Peg's face and body flashed through my thoughts, making me wonder what I was saying. "Even at my age. Joining SAP might be what they call 'Ireland's Last Hope.'"

"Looks pretty hopeless, all right," he said.

"So, a marriage to a vibrant, fiery radical is better than no marriage at all," I said.

"Now, you sound like an ignorant bachelor," Oja said. "Another one of the many."

"SAP needs to remain elite," String Bean said. "Not just anyone can join us. We need to keep racists and fools out of SAP."

"I say that we must convert those same mis-guided ones and bring them into SAP," Oja said.

"It'll never work that way."

"Then how do we gain fresh ideas?" Oja demanded. "You and I argued about this everywhere, even in bed."

"So, there!" I cracked under my breath. "The word is out."

"We can't let the opposition know our plans," String Bean said.

"What does it matter?" she asked. "Any damn fool who can read or hear knows what we want. Helping those who can't help themselves."

"Never that simple," I said. "Cliques and egos get in the way. Seeing that happen right now."

Both turned their faces to me.

"You are really a loudmouth fool, aren't you?" he said.

"If you insist."

"Bringing in this stranger, this compulsive ego-maniac chatterbox is all risk and no gain," String Bean said. "Again, I'm asking you, why tonight? What makes it so important now?"

"I wasn't in the service," I said. That was the truth. "And I never saw anyone die before." That was a lie.

"Seeing what happened to Krio tears me up," I said. "Radicalizes me. He used to talk about being in the Marines. Having to eat candy to stay awake. Maybe that caused diabetes. What did you see, anyway?"

"More than enough," he said.

"Nobody will back your entry into SAP. You'll stay on the outside. With your smart mouth and snotty jokes."

"Justin, we're not communicating the way that we used to," Oja said.

"Leave that topic alone," he said.

"Are you ashamed that we were intimate?"

"We'll talk later," he said. "In private."

He stalked across 96th Street.

Oja and I looked at each other.

"Why is it that I always push too hard?" she asked.

"Maybe because others don't push hard enough," I said.

"Sophistry," she said. "We just had some leaflets printed up very quickly, a true rush job, about Krio's death. Can you help me carry them?"

"Helping you would be charming and revolutionary fun," I said.

"Stop that," she said. "Desist with trying to win me over."

CHAPTER 15

Time for Talk
or
Lenin Never Did This

"We have a SAP van parked here," Oja said. "Our printer, Angana, did a great rush job on the flyers."

"So damn fast?"

"She is committed. As we all are."

"Committed where? Will the doctors let you out?"

"Pardon me?"

"Just a passing fancy. Take me to your leader."

She threaded her way through the crowd and down the slope of 95th Street and to a sand-colored Ram ProMaster van without windows parked on the downtown side.

To identify it later, I pressed my bare hand against the rear panel above the bumper. That was an old police trick, to leave your fingerprints on a car. Veteran cops, the kind that some call 'hair bags' had taught me that trick decades ago. These SAP radicals could switch license plates on this van and doctor the registration but my palm print would survive through all weather to identify this van later.

She knocked twice and then three times on the side panel. Remembering that code might be useful later.

The panel slid open to show two women sitting cross-legged on the van's floor.

"Sisters, this is someone who wants to join SAP," Oja said. She sounded almost shy about me. Maybe she was re-thinking her endorsement of me.

"Max," I said. "Good to meet you all. I'm embarrassed to say that I didn't know about your organization until tonight."

The van smelled of beer and something else. The something else dodged my memory. It would come to me later. Aging had taught me to wait that way.

"Max, what's your last name?" the larger woman asked. She looked like a farm woman, wide and strong. Blonde hair showing black roots hung from her head, studded by two silver pieces on her lower lip. Her silver-rimmed glasses framed a brief nose.

"Hauser," I said. "Like Kaspar Hauser."

Internet posts talked about me and my Playpen Irregulars, so I had to toss them an alias, a work name. These Sappers probably lived on their electronics. Let them check Kaspar Hauser, for kicks.

"What do they call you for short and friendly?" I asked the big blonde woman.

"We have work to do," she said.

"Okay, 'We Have,'" I said. "If that's how you want to be known."

The woman next to her, South Asian like Oja, showed a gold front tooth as she shook her head. Her jet black hair exploded from her head down her spine as she twisted to look at me.

"I printed these posters," she said in the same sprightly accent that Oja employed.

"Then you must be Angana," I said. "Pretty name."

"There he goes again," Oja said. "Mister False Face."

"Was ever a man more misunderstood?" I asked. "Wounded am I."

"We don't know anything about him, Oja?" Angana asked.

Her tone hit my nerves. She was planning something. So I had to out-think her.

"Cold out there," I said, bulling my way into the van. My two-twenty pounds rocked it.

"Hey!" Oja said. "Whatever are you doing?"

Whatever I was doing was thumbing my wallet from my back pocket out and down my pants leg into my right sock. Through winter, I always wore heavy socks outdoors. This sock held my wallet snug.

"That's fine," Angana said. "If he wants to join us —"

She gripped me by the upper arm and pulled me to her. She smelled of green mint tea and wool. Oja came beside me.

The blonde woman, We Have, slid the van door shut and the loud noise made me flinch.

The unknown scent came back to me. The smell was Hoppes gun oil. During my police years, I had used it every week to clean my Glock 9mm service gun. Someone in this van had been cleaning a gun. These lady radicals could kill me and the cops would call it a mugging gone sour.

Angana shifted her body. She blocked the door and I could not leave the van.

"Stay still," she hissed.

Her hands snaked over my belt and lower.

"Hold on, Eggnog," I said. "This is politics?"

She gripped me harder.

"Don't call me 'Eggnog!'" she hissed. "My name is Angana."

"You are nearing a controversial area," I said. "Or is this like a club initiation?"

"After we have determined that you are not a threat to us," Oja said, "we shall send some very boring, pedantic SAP members to harangue you about our creed —"

"Hold off on your harangue-utangs before sacrificing me to them," I said.

We Have leaned her body weight on me, pinning me.

Angana's hands grabbed and pulled.

The van rocked.

CHAPTER 16

Finally, a Consensus
or
For Sure, Kind Of

Oja ripped Angana's hand from my pants.

"Angana!" she hissed. "What are you doing?"

"Not sure that SHE knows," I said.

"Searching," Angana said.

"For what?" I asked. "Dominance?"

"For microphones," Angana said. "Hidden bugs. Below the belt is where they keep them."

"Among other things," I said.

"Stop fooling about, Max. And, Angana, please desist this scurrilous fumbling –"

"Wish I'd said that," I said.

"We don't need this in SAP," Angana said.

"You calling me 'this'?" I asked. "Been called better."

"Angana, he can help us reach those in his demographics."

"That's right," I said. "The whole universe is not made up of rail-thin jogging radicals under forty. Some are puffy pale fatties who will never see sixty again, like me, Our Hero."

We Have leaned harder into me.

"Hold him, Kim," Angana said.

"Why don't you just shut up?" We Have asked. "Starting now."

"Don't look now, but you're leaning on me," I said.

My back muscles scrunched under her weight.

"This is how you always got your way?" I asked. "Sitting on people?"

"Could pop your ribs right now if I wanted," We Have hissed. "Or your kneecap."

"Cancel my rumba lessons," I said. "Maybe SAP is just another political hopefuls shouting from a bully pulpit. You have your own Socialist or Trotskyite agenda, jerry-built on Deistic principles but care not one fig for this downtrodden brother murdered tonight."

"But we do!" Oja gasped. "Show you the video."

"Oja!" Angana said. "Please. That will do. No more. Remember, the Government monitors us."

"He should know."

"VIDEO? LIKE FROM THE GARAGE?" I thought.

"Don't know anything," I said. "Says so on the family crest."

"Let him freeze his buns off, handing out flyers, "We Have said. "Test his commitment that way."

"No way, Jose," Angana said.

"Isn't that phrase 'No way, Jose,' racist?" I asked. "Or, at least, stereotypical?"

"I tell you all, drop this fool. His words are strong but his vibe is wrong."

"What's that?" I rasped back. The cold, my stress and her squeezing into me hit my temper, making me lash out. "Rhymes for the revolution? I see that you're just playing with all this pointless dialectic, about whom to admit."

"That's enough of this Tomfoolery," Angana said in her British accent. "Show us some ID and we'll help you fill out an application for us."

We Have bore down on me. My ribs felt like breaking, under my winter jacket. She turned her head so she could not see me move.

My arm twisted to prevent anyone seeing the scissors jammed against my wristwatch band. As a close-up weapon, it might save me, if these idealists got violent but I did not want them to find it.

My wallet worried me as well. For a bachelor, I was sure hiding a lot of things. But that gun oil smell stayed strong in the van. Somebody radical here was carrying heat.

"Let's see who you are," Angana said. "Your papers."

"You sound like a cop," I said. "That's kind of scary."

"Well?"

"Tonight, I came out onto this frozen tundra to dance," I said. "And I never carry a wallet when dancing because it weighs me down. To dance means leaving all that behind."

"It might be wise to hold off on your joining us," Oja said.

Behind me, We Have relaxed her weight routine.

"Thank God," Angana said.

"What kind of radical says 'Thank God?'" I whined, to annoy them. "Huh, huh? Should you not be thanking Karl Marx?"

"We'll discuss your membership," Oja said in her prissy tone. "Perhaps yes, perhaps no. You can meet us at the Amity Restaurant on Madison and 84th Street at Five a.m."

"Five a.m.? When do I sleep?"

"That should test your dedication to SAP. So will passing out these flyers. They celebrate Krio's life and call for a Special Prosecutor to investigate his death."

"In this weather?"

"Absolutely," Angana said, sliding open the van door. Again, I wondered if they had a tape of Krio's death. "Now get out and work those flyers to the people to radicalize them from their routine."

CHAPTER 17

Illegal Lawyering
or
Don't Some Do It?

The SAP van door slid open and Oja and Angana pushed me back, feet-first, out into the cold.

"Hey, let's think this over," I groused. "Hate being cold."

Nancy was still standing on the corner, watching the crowd.

"Some Manhattan nights never seem to end," I said. "They just go on and on. Like tonight."

"The police are just compounding their own troubles, Mr. Royster," Nancy said. "The old line of 'Move on, there's nothing to see here,' just makes everyone think that they are covering something up."

"We agree," I said. "Let us find a warm cafe and thaw out by their radiator."

"Can't now. We're waiting for someone."

"Everyone's waiting for someone," I said. "They told me that at one of my clinics. But, why here and now? I'm icing over."

"You'll see."

"My mother used to say that to me. A very unsatisfactory answer."

"Well," she gave out in her Kansas drawl, "it's the onliest one thet you're gonna git."

The wind clawed.

We waited.

A sleek black luxury limousine slid west on 95th Street, past the conspiring SAP van. The limousine driver, jowly, fat, in his fifties, scanned us and nodded to Nancy. The side door slid open.

"Get in," Nancy said, in a different tone. Now, she sounded steely.

"Alone?"

"Get in."

"Don't wanna."

"Want to see Peg again?"

My left shin barked on the frame, getting into the limousine. A young woman with auburn hair coiled onto a shoulder and high cheekbones sat alone in the back seat. She wore an iridescent green-and-black business suit and held a pudgy black cigar in her ringed fingers.

"Scotch?" she asked in a foreign accent. It might have been Slavic.

"Weather," I answered.

"Here. No ice?"

"I'm icy enough," I said, shivering.

The Scotch warmed everything, like only whiskey can on a frozen New York night.

"Here is my card," she said. "I'm Valska, attorney-at-law. You said that you have a way to get a witness to this death into court?"

"Absolutely," I said.

My heart hammered.

"You would require compensation for this service?"

"Forty K," I said.

"That's absurd."

"Then, goodnight and thanks. I'll go to your competition."

"Wait. Paying you would breach the Canon of Ethics."

"How much do you care? Your firm sues the city, let's just say Wrongful Death, for twenty million. Or more. Right?"

"Contingent on what this witness saw."

"Your firm collects a third. Of twenty million. That's about seven mil. Forty thousand is cheap to assure that."

"We can't."

"You have subpoena forms inside that briefcase?" I asked. "Give me three blank ones. At the right time, I'll call you and you get a trial date to make it legal. You pay me and I deliver the witness to you in court."

"That's not proper subpoena service," she said.

"It is, if you care enough. I know that your firm sleeps with Supreme Court judges and tells them what to have for breakfast when they wake up. You can cuddle with them or hold them down and bugger-rape them in the middle of the night, if you choose."

"Here are your subpoenas. But you don't understand law. This won't work."

"And I need an advance of one thousand. Right now. For operating expenses."

"That makes sense, at least. I foresaw that request. Here. And please don't think that you will just take our money."

"You're advancing me cash. If I don't find the witness, do you want it back?"

"Mr. Shapiro," she said.

The driver in the front seat turned and flipped open a black leather shield case. A gold and blue-enamel NYPD detective shield dangled in the case. He was letting me see it, guessing its power, like a jungle warrior might shake his machete at the enemy or a strip-dancer might show her body.

"Retired off the Job," the driver said in a smoker's rasp. "Had this fake shield, this duplicate, made while I was still active. Fake numbers, too. Nobody can trace this tin back to me."

"Do tell?"

"Retired with seven handguns, too. And the Departmental Combat Cross. Like shooting, Royster. Always did."

"Mr. Shapiro here is one of our firm's investigators," she said. "For the past nine years. He's very effective."

"I'll just bet he is," I said. "Well- paid, too, I would imagine."

"We will find our client in Krio's family or friends," Valska said. "Someone with standing, claiming a loss, always comes forward in cases like this.

"And you are not to tell anyone about this arrangement between us."

She puffed on the cigar, making her eyes glow above the grayish smoke.

"Not nobody," the driver said.

His tone froze me to the seat so I tried looking manly and tough. But it never worked for me.

"Get out and get working," she said.

CHAPTER 18

My Plan
or
An Adult Scoffs

Nancy stood waiting for me outside the lawyer limousine. The limousine thrashed away and became another shape on the dark streets.

"Just been invited to leave two different cars," I said. "Two worlds apart. But both think that they are the cat's ass. It's the American way."

"I'd like to rep the victim Krio Yates' family against the city," Nancy said. "Why I was dirt-dumb and naive enough to try law school to start with, you betcha. Helping the weak. But I don't have the smarts, contacts or free time to take it on. City would clean my clock. What's your plan, Max?"

"You wouldn't care to know."

"Just shows to go yuh," she country-twanged. "Gotta know."

"Knowing could get you disbarred."

"By jingo, I gotta know."

"I can hear more and more Kansas in your voice. Like milk pouring from the cow to the pail. Pray tell, why must you know?"

"Because I spoke for you. Told them sharpies that they could trust you."

"Wonder if they understand that word," I said. "'Trust.'"

"Stop stalling."

"My plan is this. Leo got arrested here tonight. At his Preliminary Hearing, Leo will swear that Peg fondled him, sexwise, before the arrest. Procedure dictates that they must put a warrant on Peg for that."

"Without more evidence?"

"Yup. New law, new administration. Don't even need a name. So, knowing about the warrant, I find Peg and make a citizen's arrest. Handcuff her."

"Kinky."

"While she's cuffed, I subpoena her about what she saw tonight. The law firm pays me. Everyone's happy."

"Peg will hate you."

"She doesn't like me now. But I've got a way around that."

"Cops can bust you for Unlawful Restraint."

"To make the subpoena service valid, Valska will bribe Peg to drop the charge on that."

The crowd on the corner kept growing.

"Stop killing our brothers and sisters!" one woman wearing a Santa Claus hat wailed. "Or else, we come for you!"

"Gotta piece at home!" an Asian woman, wearing glasses, keened. "And we'll hold court right here in the streets!"

"Take it to the streets!" the crowd echoed.

"Max, please, grow up, bubba. These schemes of yours never work worth a durn. You throw together these complete fantasies and 'spect it all to come about right."

My breath sucked in.

"True that I've had a pretty long childhood," I said.

"What's wrong with you? You used to be cute and now it's just depressing."

"Not over, yet. I can do this."

"No, you can't. Look at your high muck-a-muck ego. System won't allow you, skate through it this way. You're going down and all for some love-lust little slut that you created."

CHAPTER 19

The Return of CRIT
or
Why, Now?

"You're surprising me tonight, Nancy," I said. The words tried to cover my hurt.

"Time for you to grow up some," she said.

"Reluctantly," I said, legging away from her and closer to the crowd.

"Royster!" a brief-built number in a tweed overcoat and green Alpine hat snapped. He squinted through the dark at me. Beetled brows scrunched down on piggy eyes. The face tightened.

A heavy gray scarf wrapped around the neck, keeping out the cold. The tweed coat gaped, maybe to prove that he was wearing a correct yellow necktie against his suit jacket and white shirt. His right hand held the delicate three-inch gold nugget of an NYPD lieutenant's shield. It swayed back and forth like a hypnotist's watch. The shield was a starburst design, with the city seal centered in blue enamel.

His hand holding the shield shook. An old cop story about his hand poked at my memory but drifted away.

"Whatchoo doing here, Royster?" he rasped.

"Ain't polite to ask that, Lieu," I said, using the cop-slang term for 'Lieutenant.' This was no time for me to be genteel. "Aren't you a bit long in the tooth to be DRAYDLING around crime scenes still? Whatever happened to the NYPD's mandatory retirement at sixty-three?"

"Haven't hit sixty-three yet, Royster. Just look old. Chasing humps like you ages me."

"So you say."

"Royster, wanna minute-by- minute account of what you seen here tonight. Names of who you were with."

"You mean to say 'with WHOM you were with', don't you, Lieutenant Hundshamer?"

"Don't correct my talking, you elitist snob-type. I did, best I could, you know? Didn't have your cash, good schools or anything like that."

"No cash, Lieu. Daddy Royster scratched through life as a small-time printer."

"Maybe it's time for you fancy-shmancy types to stop looking down on the rest of us."

"Are you speaking of national politics?"

"Speaking of what I'm ordering you to do, right now, without any more backtalk."

"Lieu, I'm afraid that you're just a bit behind the times here. I'm not on the Department any more."

Evers, FBI, elbowed her way through the crowd. She looked angry. An idea started in my head. An image of Peg flashed before my eyes and was gone. I had to find Peg.

"Then, you better start cooperating. Or else, I'll make sure that your pension checks keep getting lost."

"They'd have to get found first," I wisecracked.

FBI Agent Evers bobbled closer. She looked stressed. That would help my scheme.

"Say again?"

"I got no pension," I said. "You and your Irish choirboys in the Department jettisoned me off the Job without a dime."

"Why?"

"It's your own Departmental slang, Lieu. 'Terminated 'By Reason Of Disease Insanity Or Defect, Mental.' What you cops call a 'Birdie.' B-Y-R-D-I. Give someone a label like that, nobody ever has to think if it's true or not."

"With you, it's true. All my time on the Job, you the screwiest. So, give, right now."

"Why should I?"

"To save yourself a problem."

"What problem?"

"Dope it out, dopey."

"Pray, tell?"

"Royster, for a smart guy, I just dunno. I'm a decorated lieutenant. Internal Affairs, CRIT."

"I know," I said. "Notorious Lt. Hundshamer of CRIT. Critical Incident Response Team. Such a name you got. Reputation to match. Even honest cops hate you."

"Right-o, you hump. So, if I say that you shoved, threatened or obstructed me, everyone believes me. They're scared not to. You go through the system. Precinct holding cell, then a crummy chained-together-with-perps bus ride to Central Booking, drunks smelling of puke and their own you-know-what. Bus to Riker's Island. This'd be the weekend, don't see no judge till maybe Tuesday. That's if I say you did something."

"That's why some hate cops," I said. "You got that unblinking thoughtless way of handling us all."

Right now, my hidden scissor blade felt weighty against my wrist. Carrying it seemed stupid now. Hundshamer could shoot me, find the blade and claim that I had snapped my cap and attacked him with the blade.

"Few would mourn me if I vanished, Lieu. My landlord would be happy to jack up my rent-controlled apartment rate for the next sucker who comes along."

"You're spoiled, Royster. Want it all your way."

"Want to make a federal case out of it?" I asked. My voice raised.

Evers took the bait. She spun and scrutinized Hundshamer. Wind waved her hair. Her moods were changing. Now she looked feisty.

"What's this, Royster?" she asked.

"Police," Hundshamer said. "Move on."

BAM! POW! Noise filled my ears.

Shock rocked me.

Firecrackers blew. The SAP crowd hurled cherry bombs. The cops drew.

"Firecrackers!" I shouted. "Just fireworks! Everyone holster!"

Cop fingers slid to triggers. Muzzles pointed at me.

CHAPTER 20

Teaching
or
I Give the Lieu Some Law

Black Glocks pointed at me.

Nerves screamed up into my scalp.

By habit, I looked for cop bosses with gold shields and yellow uniform hat bands. Two lieutenants and a captain stood near the garage, mouths shut. The fireworks and drawn guns made them freeze. They looked scared. So did Hundshamer.

The fireworks blew behind me.

Some cop would shoot. The others would shoot, too. Psychologist called it contagious gunfire.

"Boss!" I shouted. "Holster!"

My breath sucked in.

Maybe the Academy training would work.

It worked. The cops thought that I was some unknown boss in plainclothes. The black Glock pistols slid into gun leather. Deep dark blue forearms coiled backwards like snakes and seated Glocks into holsters. Some thumbs snapped the safety catches shut.

"Facing guns twice in one night," I whispered. "Must be playing this all wrong. This IS the jazzy Manhattan late night without end."

Being scared made me chatter again.

Hundshamer and Evers and Nancy looked at me funny. They had heard me speak aloud.

"Captain!" I shouted, nerves rattling. "Control your cops!"

The captain, a moon-faced chunky, nephew of someone important in the Job, threw a hate glance my way.

"He knows by now he had lost command of these cops," I told Evers. She should see me as a pal, confiding in her about real street policing. That would lower her guard and let me con her. "I know that most of you agents never worked uniform patrol. You don't know how good cops suffer under idiot bosses like this one. But he wants to keep it a secret. Just until he can retire."

"Who tossed those firecrackers?" the captain shouted. "Lock him up!"

Some cops stepped toward the crowd, looking grim.

"Come on, ya head breakers!" a woman shouted from the crowd.

"Negative!" I hollered. My eyes locked with those of the captain. "That's just what these radical SAP kids want. Showdown. That's why they threw the firecrackers. Push your buttons and start a riot. Don't do it! Everyone stand down."

"Who the frick are you?" the captain said. His voice matched his face, shaky and scared. Both were disappointments.

"Hardly nobody," I said.

"Yeah, you are," Hundshamer said. "You're my collar. Put your loudmouth lousy hands behind your back."

My body was starting to ease up. His tone chilled me.

"That's what wrong with cops like you, Lieu," I said, stalling. My nerves needed the rest right now. "When you should be researching what happened to Krio Yates, you're blustering about WHOM you can arrest. Well, we know that you can arrest me. That's not a bulletin. But, out of cat-killing curiosity, pray tell me, on what charge d'you plan to arrest me?"

"Criminal Impersonation. You told these cops that you were their supervisor. And you're not. You're not nothing."

"Everyone is 'not nothing,'" I said. "But, before you arrest me, maybe you should check NYPL, New York Penal Law."

"No need, hump. You're in!"

"Law says you can't 'wear or display any official badge or police insignia.' And I didn't. So you can't collar me."

"You shouted 'Boss!' I heard you! The cops thought you were an NYPD boss. So you impersonated right there."

"Try convincing an Assistant DA that shouting 'Boss!' is the same as wearing or displaying any official badge or emblem, claiming to be an officer. As a matter of fact, the word 'boss' is 1960's California Beach Boys surfer slang. It means 'cool' or 'the best.' So, I was just paying your cops a compliment on how laid-back and unemotional they were. Praising them, you see."

"Bull!"

"Lieu, you usually get along with the DA's office? I doubt it. They'll never charge me on this. Everyone normal should thank me for stopping any gunfire. Your cops were about to shoot."

"Royster, buddy, I would love to blackjack you. Leave no marks nowhere. Turn your brains to jelly."

His tone turned me scared again.

"I heard that," Evers said. "Won't have you threatening my witness like that."

"Your witness," Hundshamer asked. "Who the hell, think you are?"

Evers snapped out her credentials case with the pinned FBI gold badge shining. Hundshamer had his own shield dangling from his coat side pocket.

"Oh, boy, here we go," I said. "Adults squabbling again. Battle of the badges."

"FBI, that's who," Evers said. "So, fall back."

CHAPTER 21

Professionals Chat
or
Jurisdiction Cat Fight

"Who're you, tell me 'fall back'?" Hundshamer asked Evers.

"FBI," Evers said.

"Got that, sweets. But murder ain't a federal crime. Not on any city street, anyway."

Evers assumed a face to frighten witches.

"Federal law supersedes local when there's a Civil Rights violation," she said. "That means –"

"Excuse me, Special Agent," I said.

She turned her head to snap a glare at me.

"What's your name again?" Hundshamer asked her.

She opened her mouth to answer.

"Rumpelstiltskin," I said. "Lieu, I thought that you were busy trying to arrest me. Don't get distracted by this federal sideshow."

"Royster –" Evers said.

"Lack-of-Candor," I said.

When she heard the phrase "Lack-of-Candor," Evers changed her look. She stepped about twenty feet away from Hundshamer and towards me.

"Don't give him your name," I said. "I've already forgotten it. Walk away now."

"Don't interfere. This is a Civil Rights case."

"It is," I said. "IF the US Attorney for the Southern District says that it is. Not you, an off-duty young agent with less than five years on."

"How d'you know I got less than five?"

"'cause if you had more, you would know better than to jump in like this. Or you would have stopped caring enough. It happens."

"How is it that you're telling me about my own job? D'you know more than an FBI agent does?"

"Know your limits, Evers. You can only make off-duty arrests in an emergency. And you better be 100 percent right. The rest of the time, you only act when the US Attorney's office sees a clear Federal law violation. Not before."

In the streetlight, Evers looked smaller and more vulnerable than she had before. Maybe my talk was getting through and whittling down her pride.

"Policing is a punishment-centered bureaucracy," I said.

"Sure you know that?"

"With my sparkling record, yep," I said. "Every time, took a deep breath, I got suspended again. If Hundshamer gets your name, by noon today, your boss will isolate and grill you about every syllable you uttered here on this street corner. And if he thinks that you're being less than completely honest with him, he'll file a Lack-of-Candor letter about you. And those are the letters that get you fired. Am I reading it right?"

"You must have dated a female agent, be motor-mouthing this much."

"They wouldn't have me. So, nobody's got your name. Not yet. It's time to discover geography and put it between you and this crime scene."

"There's a case here."

"But it's not yours. So, drift."

She drifted.

"Skip gets me so mad, I could kick his Cadillac into scrap," I said to Nancy.

"Yeah? Some Caddies got a safety feature for kids locked in the trunk. A kid can just kick out the back seat to escape."

"Cadillac protects the wealthy and their kids."

Rajarr the cop was still standing on the Lexington Avenue corner. Two expensive topcoats spoke to him. Hopefully, they were his union reps from the PBA union. Maybe they were muffling him.

A boxy green Dodge came down 96th Street and stopped on the corner. The cops nodded and waved him around the gray wooden sawhorse barriers. The barriers read 'Police -Do Not Cross.'

A well-fed steer of a man, old-fashioned fedora cocked on the back of his head over a hounds-tooth checkered wool winter coat, unfolded from the Dodge's front seat.

"Good evening," he said in a nasal city accent. It clashed with his slow delivery. "You look like you would know. Where's the decedent?"

"Who're you?" I asked.

"Detective Jack Hackett, Senior, NYPD Morgue Squad."

"There's a Morgue Squad?"

"Yessir. Small but dedicated."

"Never heard of you. Maybe you're a dead issue."

"Heard that one already," he said.

His face was mottled with all different shades, pale pink, red, tight skin pulled over a scar across his cheek, darkish sleepless pouches under the raisiny brown eyes and yellow-white eyebrows. The cold seemed to lash his skin. He looked like someone created from craftsmanship of a past century. He spoke of gas-light lanterns, broken down coaches and rotting harness leather.

"Hackett, lemme see your ID card."

He showed me the familiar light blue card with a dour photo of a younger Jack Hackett, Senior, in uniform. The black tie looked as if it was choking him. Lines stretched across his face in the picture. The same lines looked deeper and darker in the face before me.

"With your looks, you gotta be a civilian," he rasped out. "But, I give you the respect, just the same. Some citizens don't believe me or my shield."

"Naturally," I said.

"So the ID card eases their minds. Get it?"

"My mind could sure use some easing tonight," I said. "Thanks, Detective."

CHAPTER 22

Morgue Squad
or
Two Party Animals

The Dodge kept moving.

A round-faced steer of a man, swathed in a tweed coat with a black velvet collar, cloaked by a wool muffler the color of French dressing, rocked out of the Dodge.

"No need to check your lineage," I said. "You look just like your Pop."

"Detective Jack Hackett, Junior," the newcomer said. "NYPD Morgue Squad."

"Naturally," I said. "Where else?"

"You can cancel the wiseacre wisecracks –"

"Maybe you can," I said.

"But we got stuff to do here," Jack Hackett, Junior, breathed out, coughing against the cold. "This mess could knock New York on its ear. We gotta check the body for all kinds of stuff."

Rajarr the cop stood shook hands with his advisors. They left him alone, next to his blue-and-white patrol car. That worried me.

"Law says to wait for the M.E., the Medical Examiner," I said.

"Depends," Senior said.

"How so?"

"We're both licensed morticians, bonded by the State of New York," Junior said. He lugged out a wicked-looking black satchel from the Dodge's back seat.

"What's in that?" I asked. "The secret of life?"

"You a reporter?" Junior asked. "Lawyer? ADA? Know what an ADA is, pal?"

"Assistant District Attorney," I said. "Also known as 'A Disappointed Actor.' No, I'm none of those things."

"Private Investigator, maybe?" Senior asked. He hefted an identical black satchel from the floor. He slid a green metal plate about six inches around onto the Dodge's dashboard.

In white letters, the disc read "POLICE-NYC."

"Private investigators only worked homicides when some tycoon paid them to," I said.

"That's decades ago. Now, they hang out near Landlord-Tenants Court, disguised as real people, trying to scrape up another client to survive another rent day. Or else, they belabor slippery sidewalk cases for lawyers just as slippery. Not murders."

"Why you looking at our PD parking plate?" Junior asked. "It's legit."

Rajarr was moving sideways now, away from his car. There were no cops between him and Third Avenue now. He should not be alone now. NYPD policy said so.

"Hacketts, the last time that I saw one of those plates was in the Police Museum."

"Which is prol'ly where you figger we belong," Senior said.

"I mean, no vehicle number, no expiration date, no signature," I said. "A thing of beauty."

"Damn straight."

"And if it gets lost, nobody can trace it to any cop," I said. "Fine with me. There's too much fixation on punishment on the Job now. I oughta know. NYPD stands for 'New York Punishment Department.'"

"Like I said, work to do now," Junior said.

"No," I said.

"Huh?"

"Wait for the M.E.," I said.

"We can't. We got orders."

"They just got put on hold," I said. "LIEUTENANT!"

"The hell you doing?" Senior asked. Nothing ruffled his voice. Nothing could. Except, maybe the second coming.

"Feeding you to the Lieu," I said.

Flush from his facing off the FBI, Hundshamer hauled himself to us.

"Lieu, these two ghouls wanna hump around with Mr. Yates before the M.E. gets here," I said. "Feels like I'm tattling. But that could screw up any court case. Straighten them out, will you?"

Hundshamer took a breath.

"Are you two mutts crazy?" he began.

Rajarr walked fast towards Third Avenue. From Patrol, I knew the movement. He was taking off.

"Lieutenant!" I shouted again. "You got a runner!"

Rajarr looked back at me. He broke into a run.

"Who let him alone?" Hundshamer shouted. "Where's that idiot duty captain?"

My feet soles stung. I was running after Rajarr.

Hundshamer raced for his car.

"10-85, forthwith!" he shouted at the cops. "Suspect running."

"Call him 'suspect!'" a cop said. "That wrong, ace. He a cop!"

"Words are powerful," I panted.

"Nobody move!" some cop shouted. "Let the rats catch their own!"

"Got orders to stay here," a Latina cop screeched. "Nobody countermanded them orders."

Rajarr was crossing Third Avenue now.

Hundshamer reached his car.

Rajarr pounded his feet faster. Something fell off his belt. He kept running. Where he was going, he would not need it.

A helicopter zoomed down from above. The noise ripped, roared and covered everything like an angry God.

It could be the cops or the media.

Hundshamer threw his car forward, red dashboard light bleeding. The Hackett family gazed in funereal quiet.

The copter lit up Rajarr bounding across Second Avenue.

"This makes for great TV," I wheezed. "Clear case of someone abandoning the rule of law."

Pain knifed my chest.

"If Rajarr dies, I never see Peg again," I hissed.

Hundshamer gunned his car. Crowds blocked him.

"Let the cops run you down!" a woman caterwauled. "Show them how they treat us. Video them!"

"Whole world is watching!"

CHAPTER 23

Trying for Free
or
Why Wait?

"Whole world is watching!" someone repeated.

The crowd liked the sound of it.

"Whole world is watching!" they chorused

"Not a new chant," I whispered to myself. Running was killing my voice. "Chicago, Democratic Convention, 1968. These kids just THINK they coined the phrase."

Weather was keeping drivers indoors. For once, the First Avenue and 96th Street corner was clear.

Rajarr crossed it.

He was heading for the East River, forty feet away.

The gray waters lapped at the river walkway.

"Don't do it, kid!" Hundshamer shouted. His car WHANGED into the guardrail and stopped, too far away to stop Rajarr.

As a kid, I had pounded down beers, dodged cops on this corner and knew the turf.

Transportation used to store chains in a locked wooden shed on the walkway. Maybe they still did.

Rajarr ran lopsided now. He was just a dozen feet ahead of me. The gun belt and equipment slowed him down. That junk always stopped cops from running. And Rajarr looked like a soft puffy guy, a sports watcher, not a player.

Rajarr lunged across the walkway. My foot smashed the shed door lock. It gave.

I reached in, felt a cold chain, yanked it out and twirled it over my head like a lariat.

Rajarr threw one leg over the guardrail, six feet above the freezing water.

I flung the chain's end at him. My hand held the rest of it.

The chain caught him across the shoulders and wrapped around his chest. I yanked back. He came off the rail just as Hundshamer launched a tackle and I leaped forward.

"Yippee-kay-yay-yeh, cowboy," I wheezed.

The three of us went down in a heap together.

White light bathed us.

Too late, I saw the helicopter overhead. It banked closer.

The letters "Channel 11 News" shone on the fuselage.

"You tryinna do the Honorable Thing here?" I roared at Rajarr. Running always enraged me. "Cops kill themselves over this mess, everyone loses."

"Ain't gonna go, no jail!" he shouted. He wriggled to get free. My belly pinned him. "Six big Black greasy –"

"Cut the stereotypes," I said.

"– gonna rape me, the showers. Till I like it or they kill me."

"No more Long Island cop-fairy tales, either," I said.

"You're screwing yourself," Hundshamer said. "Running like this, dumbest flipping thing I ever seen. Where's your sergeant? Duty Captain? Procedures, supposed to prevent this kind of mess."

"I'm going Sick," he said. "Sick Leave. Gotta grant me."

The helicopter banked closer. I wondered how Channel 11 would show this onscreen tomorrow.

"Not after a suicide try," Hundshamer said.

"Why not?"

"'cause you're in. No collar. Just Mental Observation. seventy-two hours."

"No way!"

"Yep," Hundshamer said. Handcuffs snickered and clicked.

Car lights lit us up.

With mob psychology, the crowd was running towards the three of us. Manhattanites always worried that they would miss something. They were not missing much tonight.

NYPD cars followed the crowd. I rolled my gut off Rajarr's back. Hundshamer threw my lasso chain off Rajarr and stood him upright.

Someone in the crowd saw the handcuffs.

"That's the blond cop who shot him!" my SAP pal Angana shouted from the front of the mob, just where she belonged. "They're finally busting him!"

"Yay!" some others shouted.

"It's about time! Killed an unarmed Black man!"

"They're not busting me!" Rajarr shouted. "It's mental."

"Lock it up, Rajarr," I hissed. "Play this crowd. Use your head, say nothing and save it for your memoirs."

Another helicopter joined the first one. They bucked heads for a better camera angle. They swooped down so low illegally that their rotor blades blasted the East River into swirling pools.

"You just killed your own defense," Hundshamer said. He hauled Rajarr over to his car, with red light still spinning. "You better cop out, plead guilty, after this little stunt."

"Finally, I'm getting off this 96th Street," I said. "Feels like I was born and spent my life here, this whole long, one bloody night."

"Cops did right, for once!" Oja shouted from the crowd's fringe.

"That just leaves the thousands of brothers and sisters that they massacre every year."

""Thousands?" I asked. "That's wrong. Just one is too many."

"Yeah, you right!" a hefty Black man, bearded, with ugly Cazale glasses, in vogue during the Eighties shouted. "Ain't no thousands."

"Didn't the people do their job tonight?" I asked. "Upholding our Constitution."

"Yeah! Let's get on home!" another crowdster bellowed.

"Royster, where you think you're going?" Hundshamer asked. "You, you're a witness to all this. Can't just leave."

"Why?" I said. "You got cuffs on Rajarr. Got mine at home. Law says civilians can't carry cuffs. But I need them, anyway. For Peg."

CHAPTER 24

My Big Scheme
or
Childish

The cold chilled the scissors blade against my left wrist. I could feel it. The same icy tone cooled the illegal handcuffs in my hip pocket. They nested in the kind-of fake subpoena as I phoned Nancy.

"I can see that this is going to be one of Dostoevsky's White Nights, where nobody can sleep," I said to Nancy on her cell.

"Gol-dang, Max, I can sleep just fine. I'm not lovesick."

"Please get on your computer, Nancy, work those programs that show you real-life photos tonight, check these good hotels for Skip's gray Cadillac Eldorado, license 7977-AHY. These hotels should be fairly close to his Court Street office in Brooklyn."

"Why?"

"Because that will be the hotel where he stashed Peg."

"Why would Skip be in the hotel? He sent Peg away with that bodyguard lug, Joey."

"That's Skip's genius. He always gets inside his witnesses."

"Are you meaning-?"

"Just exactly what you think that I'm meaning, Counselor. That's how he wins so many cases. He lives with his witnesses. Charms them, tells them how great they are. His witnesses love him. If they are any kind of a woman, he will woo them and do everything except take them into bed. Sometimes, he breaks that rule and beds them."

"Could disbar him for that."

"If they ever catch him. Since he got his law ticket, he broke every law except the law of gravity, get himself disbarred. Nothing ever seems to stick. Witnesses move, forget or recant."

"D'you think that he'll seduce Peg?"

"Maybe she'll plank him. We got two hustlers hustling each other here."

"But you're falling for her?"

"Gotta see where this goes."

"Goes bad, Max. Think I can promise you that. Won't Joey stay with Peg? Maybe in the same hotel? Share a room with Skip?"

"Because Skip works without witnesses. Someday, Joey might have to turn on Skip, to save himself. And he'll claim that Skip bribed or tampered with Peg as a witness."

"Do they call that 'tampering'?'"

"Skip can't risk that. Once Peg is inside her hotel room, Skip will send Joey home. Call him back when needed."

"Why the Sam Hill Joey risk jail, doing all this?"

"Because Joey looks and acts like a prison inmate to me. They have a certain aura, if you been around them enough. I have. Some hooligan lawyers like Skip hire convicted felons on lifetime parole for murder or rape. They actually approach the Parole Board and promise to employ the inmate as a chauffeur, law clerk or office assistant. The Parole Board sees this as a way to stop feeding this lifer. On paper, this lifer working for a lawyer like Skip looks good. So they agree."

"Why does Skip go through all this?" she asked.

"To own a slave. If Joey ever angers Skip, Skip can call Parole and say that Joey stole office petty cash or threatened Skip or did any kind of crime at all. The state will believe a lawyer like Skip, revoke Joey's lifetime parole at a half-hour hearing and sling him back into prison, probably forever. So, Joey obeys Skip in everything. His life depends on it."

"I'm gonna give you his favorite hotels."

While I fidgeted from nerves, I read her off the hotel list.

"Never heard of most of these. They're near his office."

"And new. Brooklyn is changing now. Red Hook, Gowanus and Carroll Gardens are sprouting new hotels because Brooklyn is hot with travelers now. Like Greenwich Village used to be."

"How d'you figure that he'll drive and not take a cab there?"

"Because I know Skip. Worked for him. He hates cabs. Loves driving his very own Cadoo. Says, 'Hey, man, don't scratch up my per-son-ality.' And he's got his own toilet kit, razors, fresh shirt, socks and drawers in that Cadillac trunk. He'll take his own room in the hotel, for legal discretion reasons. If there's a squawk about him gaffing the witness or the client, he can always prove that he took a separate room. Paid with a card, leaving a paper trail."

"While I'm working my gol-danged computer, what'll you be doing, justify your pay?"

"Freezing," I said. "Outdoors."

I did. Digging down deep for cash, I took a yellow cab to those same Brooklyn hotels. Nancy's computer could not penetrate darkness. If Skip had parked away from streetlights, his Cadillac might not show on the screen.

Or, the screen might show older useless photos.

My driver was a woman about 30, with glossy dark hair and a singsong accent.

"Rare such cold wea-ther my Bangladesh country, sir," she said. "My husband has flu. So I must work nights."

"Pretty risky, nights," I said.

"We Muslim wives must obey the husband. Sorry that my heat-er is not working, sir. Are you looking for a friend at these hotels?"

"No friend. My wife."

"Your wife, sir?"

"Maybe some day."

CHAPTER 25

Hunting by Night
or
Suffering for Peg

As my cab rattled past Brooklyn hotels, I read my driver's name off her hack license: Tanzin Bari.

"Ms. Bari," I asked. "Might we turn on the TV here, in the front seat?"

"Oh, yessir. Straight away."

The TV screen showed an aerial shot of Lexington Avenue and East 96th Street.

It felt like I had never left that corner.

"Authorities are still trying to solve the mystery of what happened down this garage ramp," a stylish Asian woman reporter with close-cropped hair said. "Did the dead man, Krio Yates, try to grab the gun from Police Officer Wendell Rajarr?"

The camera showed the garage ramp again. Hundshamer passed by it, looking like a mean Protestant preacher.

Maybe this tape was old. Maybe three hours old. Or perhaps tonight was grinding me older.

"Legal experts differ on whether Officer Rajarr committed a crime by attempting to flee," she continued. "Certainly, as an officer, he could not evade Departmental procedures and hope to keep his job. PBA President Brendan Faye had this comment."

The screen showed a slim, spectacled man, with a bald head, standing outside the 19th Precinct, where I had often gotten suspended while trying to serve.

"The public always rushes to judgment on any police shooting, " he said. A faint Irish brogue flavored his speech. "Until proven otherwise, we stand in support of Wendell Rajarr. By the way, his nickname among his brother officers is 'Wendy.' Does 'Wendy' sound like the nickname of a brutal or heavy-handed officer?"

The camera shifted to my SAP pal Angana.

"We demand a Special Prosecutor investigate this murder!" she shouted. "How can we trust an officer who tries to flee justice? He threw away his gun, to hide evidence!"

"Some say that his fleeing, as you call it, was a suicide attempt," the TV reporter said. "And that was a replacement gun, while they examined the one fired. Standard procedure."

"Fleeing is fleeing. Whether to Brazil or the hereafter," Angana said. "If you were innocent, would you kill yourself?"

Tanzin drove me past a new hotel overlooking the Brooklyn Heights promenade.

Skip's Cadillac, the one with the kick-able trunk, had to be somewhere, I told myself. But it was not here.

My thumb switched the TV screen to Channel 32 BJ Lightning News.

Skip's bulk showed onscreen.

He stood in front of an apartment building. There was no number on the building. Something crashed behind him.

"This just follows the chain of police shootings nationwide," Skip was saying. "Where White cops gun down unarmed Black men. Ferguson, Missouri, and North Charleston, South Carolina. Chicago, Los Angeles and many more, all covered up. We cannot allow more of this here in New York. Killing a former US Marine! If necessary, we must show the rest of the country how to police the police."

"Do you speak for the victims in these shootings?" a Black woman reporter, full-figured and stolid, asked Skip, holding the microphone under his chin.

"Absolutely."

"At last count, you earned a three million dollar judgment against New York in the Quincy Durwood, Junior, death lawsuit."

"Did I?" Skip asked. "That seems to matter more to you than to me."

On the screen, there were no numbers or landmarks behind Skip. He could be anywhere, dallying with Peg.

The story ended.

The station reported on a dog show at Madison Square Garden.

My fingers stabbed the Channel 32 BJ Station Hot-Tipz toll-free number.

"Channel 32 BJ Station Hot-Tipz," a youngish man's voice said. "What's the story?"

"I'm a World War Two veteran," I lied. "Combat Engineers. And one of your camera crews just saved my dog's life, that's my Rutherford, a Char-Pei, all that I got left and I want to thank you all."

"Yessir," he said. "Where did this happen?"

"That's what I want to ask you. I'm just visiting here from Fresno. Don't know your streets. My home health aide, Rupert, already went to sleep. So, can't tell you."

"Sir, in that case —"

"Except the driver had a lady passenger, front seat. Big Black woman, about thirty-five. She just was talking to a fat Black guy across from my building. Don't you think your cameraman deserves some kinda reward?"

"That would be Stella Grissom, our reporter," he said. Playing detective pleased him. "Hold on and I'll get where she was working. Then, we'll send the van out to you for a stand-up interview with you, sir. Okay?"

He went away.

I felt like my heart was sawing through my pink chest flesh.

CHAPTER 26

Not Subtle
or
Now, A Night Action

My driver Tanzin whirled us down another Brooklyn Heights side street. The Viceroy, a new hotel, took up the corner.

"No garage, Tanzin," I said. "And I don't see my friend's car."

She did not answer.

Her dark head with under a pink bonnet against the cold looked out the window. Her lips pursed. Maybe she was day dreaming about home in Bangladesh.

"Did you hear me, Tanzin?"

Tanzin did not answer. She was in her own world.

"You shouldn't be out driving tonight," I repeated.

Station 32 BJ Station Hot Tipz swung back onto the phone, with the fast accents of today's Younger Generation.

"Yes sir," he said. "Absolutely. Like, we checked what you said and that van went to 11 Ferris Street in Brooklyn. Red Hook neighborhood, actually."

My cold cheeks pushed out as I grinned to myself.

"11 Ferris Street, you say?" I asked, just to make sure.

"Uh-huh. Will you want to, like, set up an interview thing with us now?"

"Not now, son. All tuckered out. I'll call you back in the morning for that interview. Okay?"

"Yes sir, that's a wrap. Okay."

He was not concerned. His voice had that 'Yeah, whatever, dude, 'I'm-back-on-my-computer-anyway,' tone that I often heard.

"Ferris Street, please, Tanzin," I said. "Go across the Gowanus Canal, near Buttermilk Channel, into Red Hook."

"Red Hook, sir?"

"Brooklynites call this area of docks, wharves and warehouses 'Red Hook' 'cause the land forms a hook. Got no subway station, cuts it off from the city. Just one city bus line runs through the neighborhood. Kinda from time to time."

"I understand, sir."

"Tanzin, views of the city skyline and New York Harbor had always thrilled me in Red Hook," I babbled on, from nerves again.

"For decades, Red Hook had lived as its own little universe. Tight-lipped longshoremen, blue collar workers and small-time Mafia foot soldiers had peopled Red Hook. Normals shunned it as a secret, dangerous and grimy world. The Red Hook housing project suffered brutal murders.

"Now the New Brooklynites have discovered it, built an IKEA furniture store and shopping mall. The street we're going to may have a hotel, too new for an Internet posting. Pretty soon, we'll see."

We crossed over the brooding Gowanus Canal and into Red Hook.

My fingers touched the scissors again, wedged under my wristwatch. Maybe it was a silly weapon to trust but I wanted something to cut if needed. And no cop would arrest me for carrying scissors.

From back in memory, I could imagine some corrugated desk sergeant, hash marks showing decades of service, counseling this arresting cop who might dare to arrest Our Hero, me, for carrying this weapon.

"A scissors, huh, Officer?" the old Sarge would rail.

"And whose did he stab wid it? Try to slice up some nice taxpayer? Is this a Deadly Instrument as enumerated in the New York Penal Law? Is it listed as a dagger or a dirk or a dangerous knife? I think not. Now, why don't you just kick this rascal loose out the precinct back door and pray that he doesn't find some buck-hungry lawyer to sue you and me and steal our pensions?"

For months, I had heard that kind of talk at the precinct front desk.

Our cab hit a pothole and jolted me back to now.

Maybe I was getting cynical. I hoped so. Something made me fret that this Ferris Street address had come too easily for me.

So I tapped the bulletproof partition separating Tanzin and myself.

"Tanzin, if I recall rightly, Ferris Street is right around this corner," I said. "So, stop here, please, and let me off. Here's thirty dollars to cover the meter so far and for your trouble."

"Thank you, sir. Therefore, I can stop working for tonight."

"Yep. Please wait here in your cab and let me walk in first. If everything is okay, I'll come right back and we'll figure out our next move."

"I understand, sir."

"Just stay here. Don't drive onto Ferris Street right now. You would stand out too much. There's no other yellow cabs around this gritty tough neighborhood, this time of night. Even with the yuppies nearby. So, just park here."

"Okay, sir."

She stopped and I left the chilled cab onto the colder street.

Ferris Street loomed up ahead. My pulse pounded again. Tonight was tearing me apart again.

Ferris Street seemed dead quiet in the frigid air.

The corner showed me nothing.

Behind me, Tanzin's cab jerked forward and drove past me onto Ferris Street.

"Tanzin!" I shouted. "Stop!"

She took the corner.

BAM!

Something exploded. Panicked, I dropped flat.

CHAPTER 27

Why?
or
Frozen Forensics

My insides scrambled. I ran to Tanzin's cab.

Something pushed me closer to her. Broken glass shone. The cab skidded. It slammed into a pole. The back window was out. Tanzin turned from the steering wheel. Her face twisted.

"You okay?" I yelled.

"Yes sir," she said.

"'Yes sir,'" I quoted her. "Always polite. That's British breeding at work."

My eyes hop scotched over her body. Often, shock hit victims. They could not say if they were hurt. That came later. It had happened to me like that. Tanzin showed no blood anywhere on her body.

Yanking open the cab's back door, I looked for spent bullets and sniffed for cordite. It wasn't that kind of movie. A squarish grey rock lay on the back sear

Someone had tossed it through the window.

A figure moved across Ferris Street. He ran, hiding his face with his hands. It looked like Skip's bodyguard, Joey. He must have thrown the rock.

I played my hunch.

I hollered.

"Joey!" I shouted. "Stop or you and me gonna dance!"

Joey danced without me. He ran down the street. He moved fast, for a side of beef.

I made sure that his hands were empty. Or else he might gun me into Lonely Lovers' Heaven.

He zigzagged into an alley. Joey had maybe grown up on broken-bottle alleys like this one. He looked it. On the other hand, Mother Royster had kept me indoors, reading books and avoiding the Bad Element. So he had me beat in Bad-Boyness.

Something solid hit my shin. That stopped me.

"Oh, showers of bastards!" I sang out.

Hopping on one leg, my body jiggled its load of muscle, bone and fat.

"Never happened to James Bond," I wheezed.

Something moved near me.

Joey might double back to finish me.

My fingers scrabbled at my wrist. The scissors-dagger came out in my fist.

I lunged toward the noise.

The scissors-dagger pointed dead ahead, to stab Joey in his belly.

A fat gray possum, complete with beady pink eyes, jowls and dewlaps, looking like a banker, gawked at me.

By reflex, my scissors dagger lanced out at him. The blade missed him. His paw went out and caught me at the right wrist. I could feel the nails slice my skin.

They felt like razors. Pain stung me.

"I'm gonna say a terrible word!" I bellowed.

The possum sneered at me. He turned with great gravity to show me a broad gray haired rump.

I kept busy leaping backwards.

He waddled away under a cardboard box and out of my life, I hoped.

Cold stung my hurt wrist.

Still moving away from my newest pal in the animal kingdom, I galloped after Joey.

Up ahead, a car coughed alive.

That gave me a glimpse of Skip's gray Cadillac charging down the side street. Joey's pale face showed at the wheel. He looked scared.

He drove like it.

Skip's Cadillac zigzagged and skidded across the street.

I hoped it would crash.

Raging, I flung my scissors- dagger at the car. It was stupid. Knife-throwing only worked in the movies. It never killed anyone. But, like everyone else, movies had ruined me for real life.

The scissors pinwheeled and flew twenty feet from the car. It bounced off another parked car and slid into the gutter.

"Couldn't get more stupid," I muttered.

Bending down to pick it up, my hand shook. I saw that it was snapped in two. One blade was gone. I searched but did not see it. The remaining blade lay on the concrete, bent but still okay. I straightened out the blade by pressing all my weight between it and the curb. It held a bend to the left now but it would work and I slid it back under my wristwatch band.

My hand reached back to my belt for the handcuffs. They were gone.

"O, showers of varlets!" I shouted. "A great detective!"

The cuffs must have fallen from my belt when I ran. To-night, I was fast losing weapons.

Again, searching got me zilch. Darkness won.

"Now, all I got against Peg is my body," I said.

By the time I limped back wheezing and coughing and searching, to the cab, Tanzin was crying. Tears sprang from her exquisite eyes and scored her face.

"Cannot pay for the window, sir!" she wailed. "'tis quite dear!"

"Expensive, you mean," I said. "More British English."

"Oh, sir!" she gasped. "You are hurt!"

She stared at my right wrist.

The possum nails had found my skin and sliced it. Four gashes of blood showed in the streetlight.

"In my mirror, I see the man throw something," she said. "Now he hurt you."

"He put up a helluva fight but he got away," I said.

"Now, what can I do about this window?" she said. "Sadir, my husband will just die."

She kept crying.

I joined her.

"But, sir, why are you crying?"

"Dunno. Maybe Peg softened me."

"Pardon?"

"Let's both stop crying," I said. "I've got a plan."

CHAPTER 28

Civil Service
or
What, Me Lazy?

With me pointing, Tanzin drove us with the shattered rear window lancing frigid air all over us.

"Frozen nights like this, you wonder how the Dutchmen chose such a cold grey mess of a place to start a city," I said, just to keep talking.

"Money," Tanzin said.

"Well put, Tanzin. You're full of surprises tonight."

"Bad black night."

"You're right about that, too. Sure a long one, anyway. The kind that you train for, your whole life. Money seems to drive everyone tonight."

"Why he throw that thing?"

"Dunno. Maybe he's in love. People in love will do anything. Here's Union Street. Home of the valiant 76th Precinct. Let us enter to palaver with them."

"No police."

"They can't hurt you, deport you, or anything like that."

"Yes sir. No police."

"Why not?"

"My friend fall in the sidewalk. Police come, ambulance. Ambulance people do not like foreigners, call Immigration, ICE, get my friend put in detention facility, maybe sent back to Bangladesh."

"They can't do that."

"Did it."

That took care of that.

"Tanzin, that rock really scared me," I said. It was the truth. "I have a heart problem." Now, I was lying, to get her help. "That attack made my heart disease worse. So, I need a police report to show that it really happened. That way, I can get my medicine for my heart. Or else, the next attack might kill me."

"Police make me afraid."

"Me, too, sometimes."

Now I was back walking the truth trail again.

The 76th Precinct building looked squatty and gray. An air of punishment hung around it. The blue-and-white Radio Motor Patrol cars, what cops called RMPs, lay cold and gleaming. They were double-and-triple parked on the curb. Nobody wanted to walk in this hellish weather.

Inside was a high brown wooden desk, with a bored-looking Latino cop with Union-plan black glasses over a nose bent broken to the left. His nameplate read Olak.

"Yup?" was his greeting to us taxpayers. Tanzin squirmed.

"Someone threw a rock at our cab," I said. "Ix-nay on the back window. Saw this man Joey running after the rock was thrown."

Nothing stirred on the cop's wide face.

"Let's go, sir," Tanzin said.

She turned to the door.

"D'you want me dead from a heart attack?" I asked her.

Her face knotted. Now, she looked older. She stopped walking towards the street.

"Didja see him throw it?" Olak asked. His voice held a country twang to it, rare in a New York City cop. He might have been from upstate, in the farm areas. You could live anywhere and test for the NYPD. One cop that I had worked with came from the Canadian border.

"Just running afterwards," I said. It sounded weak to me. "But I know he did it and his name's Joey and I want a warrant put out on him for Criminal Mischief."

"'Criminal Mischief', huh? You were on The Job?"

"Guilty."

"Got your retired shield?"

"Didn't retire."

"Yeah? What happened?"

"Would depress you."

"Why?"

"Depresses me."

"You didn't see him throw it, pal, not much I can do."

"He could have killed us both," I said. My face warmed with our talk, after the frost outside.

"Shoulda, woulda, coulda," he chanted.

"I'm requesting a warrant on this mope Joey."

"No can do. You're not hurt or nothing."

"Look here," I said. My wrist was still bleeding from where the opossum had sliced me. "From the window glass. Where it broke."

"Looks like a cat scratch to me."

"You're an animal forensic expert now. Sergeant here?"

"On patrol."

"No desk sergeant? Try again."

"Toldya, on patrol."

"Lieutenant?"

"Out sick."

"Okay. Ambulance and the Duty Captain."

"Ya don't want that."

"Indeed I do."

"You could get locked up, ya know."

"Pray tell, why?"

"Perjury. Or he could claim, YOU hit him." He looked at Tanzin. "You and your boyfriend could get arrested. You see this thing or what?"

"Sir, I am driving. I see not a thing."

"You see?" he asked.

"I see ambulance and Duty Captain. Or a report naming Joey employed by Skip Cossee, 26 Court Street, Brooklyn. And a copy of the report for her taxi insurance."

"Who is she to you? You giving her the old tap-tap or what?"

"PO Olak. Warrant."

"She looks kinda shaky."

"Your mother looks kinda shaky. Now, scratch out that report."

"Or what?"

"Or I take this out of this precinct and right to Internal Affairs. They have my chair all ready and waiting there. And I curl up in their lap and sing them songs that you will hate to hear."

"You threatening me with Internal Affairs?" Olak asked. "The headhunters? The rat squad."

My stomach corkscrewed again. Olak was right. Feeding him to Internal Affairs felt grimy.

I did not know what to do.

CHAPTER 29

Marriage Counseling
or
Bodies Rasp

Tanzin drove me from the 76th Precinct house.

She had the UF-61 police report folded into her red and orange beaded shoulder purse.

"Tanzin, you should take yourself and your broken window taxi home now," I said.

"Please drop me near the Hyatt in Brooklyn Heights. I'll score another cab there."

"Yessir."

We drove.

"You're driving towards the water," I said. "Brooklyn Heights and all those straight-limbed Anglos with their trust-funds, they're over there."

She did not answer. No more 'Yessir.'

"Tanzin?"

She steered us to a stretch of street near the piers. The black water shifted past, holding more of the city's secrets. She stopped the car.

"What's the buzz, here?" I asked.

"Why we stopping here? You planning to throw me in?"

She slid out of her door, opened the back and sat next to me.

"When the window break, I am so scared," she said. "I cannot drive now."

"Want me to try? Believe me, you don't."

"My husband, he change religion last year," she said. "Now, he does not touch me."

"Bet you say that to all the single millionaires."

"Not nothing, never. Don't know what to do. So, I touch you now. Nice?"

"I know some good lawyers."

"Please, sir, stop making funnies."

"You're asking a lot."

"Does this feel good, sir?"

"Too damn good. Remember that you're still married. Have you talked to him?"

"Cannot, sir. Want to talk with you, sir."

"Do you think that's a good idea? Did you ask your doctor?"

"Silly."

"Who? Me, or your doctor?"

"Augh?"

"Maybe both," I said.

"Please, sir."

"Tanzin, all I know about this love stuff is that I don't know much about this love stuff. Whatever 'tis, might be happening to me with someone I just met."

"Is a woman?"

"That's the rumor."

"Where is she?"

"And that's the question."

Tanzin wound herself around me. She smelled of scented lemon soap and clean linen. Her mouth smeared mine and kept pushing.

"It's true what they say," I said. "In this Manhattan night that never ends, you stay out past your bed-time and all kinds of lust finds YOU."

She had been eating something with mint in it tonight.

"Dear lady," I tried saying. "Let us reevaluate –"

"You good –"

"I like the way you talk, Mrs. Bari," I said. "But larger issues loom here."

"You try to say?"

"I may be falling for someone else. You remember when you first knew that you loved your husband?"

"Marriage by families talking."

"D'you mean an arranged marriage?"

"Is my culture."

"That sure cancels the hell outta my question about when you knew that you loved him. But, okay. Experts say when you're in love, you give off a happy glow. Others can feel it. It attracts those others. Maybe you're feeling that around me now."

She moved against me again, then backwards.

Her fingers opened her coat and the heavy wool shirt underneath. Her rose-colored bra fell. She showed me her body, dark and writhing in the cab's half-light. She slid to me.

CHAPTER 30

Real Danger
or
Married Life

"Hating to sound passé," I said, "nevertheless, you are married, my dear."

"He forget."

"Then you should remind him. Get him pounding down whiskies, talk dirty to him. Watch risqué Japanese films cuddled up together. If he finds you cheating, he may kill you."

"Wouldn't."

"Or his brother might. Honor killing. Blood feuds. Read about them in penny-dreadful books about Doctor Fu Manchu,"

"I care not so much now."

"Takes time. How many children d'you have?"

"Three."

"They don't need a death or a divorce on life's great stage. Why do you choose me, at my age, with all my legions of problems?"

"You okay."

"Not exactly Mr. Right. You're going through a problem time now. And you have to take steps to repair it. I would just distract you."

"You use your brains, find many reasons, tell me no."

Her voice trilled, with her foreign cadences.

"Marriage matters. If you want to stop the marriage, you can always do that. Lawyers are standing by. But make sure first."

"They just words, yes?"

"More intelligent than most of my gobbling."

"May we just stay here, peaceful?"

"Tanzin, I would like that. But, human nature and me being what they are, one thing would surely lead to another."

"Few minutes?"

"If I stay, I may miss seeing my beloved, forever and forever. Lose that chance, my SAP stuff and my own self-respect."

She gaped at me.

"Sorry," I said. "Didn't mean to preach."

My cellphone played "The Flower Duet" from Delibes' opera LAKMAE.

"Wake me, shake me," I said into the phone. "You just saved my virtue."

"Riilly?" Nancy, on the phone, asked in her Kansas twang.

Tanzin grinned. She showed teeth like young pearls, making silly goo-goo eyes, convinced that I was flirting with some blonde Hollywood starlet suffering from loneliness by the poolside.

"Yes. My virtue. That old thing."

"SAPPERS talk to me," Nancy said. "They know that I share some of their values."

"You do?"

"Some, Mr. Royster. Just some. And the SAP ones I know did not go to Krio Yates' death scene tonight. They stayed warm in bed."

"Sensible folk," I said.

"So, they did not see you and I together. But they talk. They tell about the hefty old stranger at the scene. Some suspect you of informing on them."

"To whom? Who the devil would care what these misguided, overeducated children think or do?"

"They do. Paranoia empowers them, makes them feel important. They could trap you somewhere and hurt you."

"These bookworm-joggers will send out death squads if they suspect that I blowed on them?"

"It already happened," Nancy said. "A youngster named Syonge mixed with them and made fun of their ideas with the Manhattan Chronicle giveaway paper. Syonge just vanished. Nobody ever saw him after that."

"Could be stringing coral seashells in Tahiti," I said.

"Was just twenty-two, hated travel, never lived anywhere but Manhattan and had a family and a girlfriend that he loved."

"Love, again. Seems hard to get away from that mess tonight."

"Don't forget sex," she said. "And idealizing. Or codependency."

"Got someone who's husband fell out of love with her," I said. "You take cases to pay for bailing out your lover-man, Santiago, the crack dealer. And I'm freezing all across the city, hunting love."

"Max, you're a windbag."

"Okay, I buy it," I said. "SAP kids can kill. But, I gotta see if they can video. They might crack this case wide open. So, I have to meet them."

"If I never see you again —"

"Check the cheaper massage parlors in Heaven," I said. "I'll be working there as the Towel Boy."

That ended our talk.

The wind blew again, cutting my skin.

It made me want to curl up somewhere warm.

Tanzin lifted her liquid eyes onto mine. Her jaws worked and her throat pulsed. She said nothing.

"Go home, Tanzin," I said. "Hug the family for me."

CHAPTER 31

Switching Drivers
or
Style Clash

Brooklyn Heights looked desperate cold. Nothing stirred on Adams Street. Nobody walked.

Further down the street, murderous prisoners dozed in cells, guarded by underpaid Bureau of Prisons officers. I knew that they felt the same cold clawing at them under the blankets made by Unicor, doing business as Federal Prison Industries. Those same blankets had swaddled me in jail for a while and I recalled how scratchy they felt.

No headlights meant no cabs or limousines.

"This gets serious for our hero," I gritted through my teeth. "I'm not going to trudge across this frozen tundra on foot tonight."

Headlights washed over the street.

"City never sleeps," I said. "Yonder my ride."

A sleek black Lincoln Continental eased down Adams Street towards me. My hand lifted up to hail him.

"Yeah?" The driver showed a reddish face pinked by the cold with a grey cavalry moustache. He leaned out the driver's window, scanning me.

"Howya doing? I need to check the hotels near here for my brother's Cadillac. He forgot something important at work."

"Gonna take a while."

"No way. Only about eight or nine hotels near here. New ones. It's the Brooklyn Renaissance."

"Two hundred."

"Two hundred hotels? Huh? Like the Frank Zappa song? What are you talking?"

"Two hundred bucks to take you around the hotels."

"Awww," I said in a monotone. "You have heat-stroke. But I will call you an ambulance."

It was an old line. My Uncle Dinny used to give it to bartenders when he saw his bar tab.

This driver ripped open his door and got halfway out. His wide face worked mad. He swung a gray lead pipe. In the light, some dried blood colored the pipe's end. He was going to add my blood there.

"GET BACK!" I shouted.

My heel caught his open door and kicked it shut. The door caught him across his leg.

"Sneaky mother –"

"How right you are," I panted. "No fair more fights, this Senior Citizen. Stay there. Or you'll get bad, mad hurt."

"You just wait there, player!" he shouted.

"Not my plan," I said.

"Beat your fat face in!"

"Come on," I said. My right hand palmed the scissors-dagger and I held it at gut level. Maybe he saw it, maybe not. By now, I did not care anymore.

"See you fronta me, BOOM!" he said. "Hit and run dead! See you in the graveyard, ya fruitcake."

"Your mother wrestles main events," I said. "Granny holds the spit bucket."

He folded back into his limousine. It lurched away and down the frosty street.

"Charming fella," I said. "Can hardly wait for the next contestant."

Winter visitors to New York delighted in the crisp clear air. They could have it. I wanted some sweltering sweaty July heat right now.

The cold kept burning into me.

"I could just stay here and keep freezing," I said aloud. My breath plumed. "Just like there was no Peg, no Krio Yates nor Skip. Or forget the whole mess and fall into one of these hotel rooms with central heating and thick wool blankets on the bed. That's the logical, adult thing to do. The kind of plan that would make Nancy happy."

A homeless Latino man huddled in a sleeping bag on a bench. Two Black cops were standing heavy- footed and solid nearby.

"Not going into no shelter tonight," the homeless man was saying. "And the law just changed. Lawyers told us. You can't make me, go the shelter."

"You're right, bro,'" the younger cop. "Can't make you. New laws. This cold will kill you. We used to be Fascists. Now we're murderers."

Another limousine, a Buick, with NYC Taxi and Limousine Commission plates, came down the street. Behind it, the Brooklyn Bridge gleamed like a chain of pearls slung across the black velvet night.

The chill made my hands go up fast to flag him down.

"Heya!" he shouted. His shaved head and glasses gleamed. About five-eight, 250 pounds and 30 years old.

"Not supposed to pick up anyone on a street hail. Two thousand dollar fine. Where d'you want to go?"

"Check some hotels. Looking for a car. Okay?"

"All right. Flat rate? Fifty bucks? Get in. Cold out here."

"I'm cynical. What's your name?"

"Orville. Y'know? Like the Wright brothers."

"Deal, Orville. Let's try the St. George on Henry Street."

We swung that way, across the Kings County Supreme Court plaza.

A gray shape came from the side street and sped in front of us.

My head jerked upright.

"That's the car, Orville! Please tail him."

Orville gunned it. We drew closer.

The light up ahead changed. The Cadillac went through it.

"If I blow the light, he'll see it," Orville said. "Might tumble to us."

"Take it."

Orville scanned the street and eased through the red light.

Sixty feet ahead, the Cadillac bucked and shot forward.

"Now he's running!" I said. "Don't lose him now!"

CHAPTER 32

Fantasy
or
Hotel Detective

Orville handled his car like a crash pilot, turning his head to check for traffic and ripping through intersections.

"We'll snatch this fool up!" Orville chortled.

With his weight, age and impatience, Orville would die young.

The Cadillac zoomed ahead, tore corners apart and straightened out. Orville swung us after him. The turn made my guts swim inside me.

It reminded me how hungry I was.

We missed a pickup truck by inches.

"O, showers of bastards!" I cried out.

"Chill out, man," Orville said. "Got it made in the shade."

"I must be crazy in lust," I said to myself.

The Cadillac flew down a slim street, sparked orange on the undercarriage and was gone again.

"Hot spit!" Orville shouted out. "He dumped us!"

We tore up and down other streets. The Cadillac had vanished again.

"Not your fault, Orville," I said. "Here, some coffee cash."

"No way, Jose. I lost him, I don't take your money. A pride thing, you know? I'm a pro."

We rode to two more bed-and- breakfasts in Cobble Hill.

In the back of my head, I kept remembering how much Skip enjoyed the St. George Hotel. He and I had always stashed surprise witnesses there and walked them in disguises to Brooklyn Supreme Court a few blocks away.

Orville's phone played Nutcracker music. Christmas was coming. He scooped up the phone.

"Hey, hey," formed his greeting.

He listened.

I kept scanning.

"Roger dodger all that," he said and ended the call.

"Gotta paying job, Manhattan," he said. "Kids and their clubs. All looking for love."

LIKE ME, I thought.

"These kids today," I said. "I tell ya."

It was a corny old line from vaudeville.

"So, I gotta go pick them up, carry them home," he said. "Sorry."

"Drop me by the subway," I said. "And take this green. Or else, I'm insulted."

He did not insult me.

The subway entrance looked like a frozen doorway to the Antarctic. SKIP'S IN THE SAINT GEORGE, I told myself.

Somehow, I sensed it.

On all cases, from missing teenagers to murder defense, Skip had always schooled me with one rule. That rule was: Go with your gut.

I went with my gut across the frozen Columbus Park and onto Henry Street.

The Saint George Hotel had its own security, a reedy youngster in his twenties who was watching the street outside when I came inside the front door.

"Gerry, how the hell are you?" I asked. "Remember me? Skip Cossee's legman. Max Royster. Skip wants a report as soon as I get here. No matter what time."

"Sure, I remember you," Gerry said. He did not sound sure.

"You helped us a lot, keeping those wits under wraps in here," I lied. "Skip talks you up all the time. Got you lined up for some real sweet Executive Protection slots next month."

Gerry grinned. He lived in his fantasy, seeing himself as a young James Bond, now learning his craft as a hotel guard. It was the same dream that I used to have, before I wised up.

"Just doing my job."

That phrase always rankled me.

"Got another one now. Skip said that you'd point me to the room," I said, trying to sound routine.

My breath went in. This was a big roll of the dice.

"You sure?" Gerry said. "I don't know about that."

"Okay," I said. "Just show me your registry."

"No can do. New manager jerk-o slapped controls onto our registry. Need to send an email to our parent company. Then, they decide, once they check with their vice-president for Information —"

"Jesus wept," I said. "Forget all that high-tech linoleum-talk that means nothing. Just tell me this, Gerry. Who had steak-and-kidney pie and rice pudding ordered to their room tonight?"

"Why?"

"'cause that's what Skip lives on, late night, like now."

"Serious?"

"Serious as a heart attack. What room?"

"Can't."

"Respect your discretion but meals aren't confidential. Executive Protection. Travel, hot women —"

"Suite 308. Our biggest. Bedroom, kitchenette."

Creaking upstairs, I found 308 and tapped on it.

Skip would never answer a nighttime knock.

"Gerry here, Mr. Wade," I said. My voice imitated Gerry's whine. Getting Skip to open the door would take some real conman hustle. "Got somebody here with some pictures. About some cop shooting a guy."

Skip usually washed down dinner with three or four Martinis. That might cloud his judgment, blended with greed.

The door opened a crack.

Pushing off the floor with my foot, I shoved all of my weight against the door.

It gave inward.

Skip slopped backwards into the large suite.

"Talk low," he whispered. "Peg's asleep here. She keeps talking about you."

Everything in me jumped.

"In bed," Skip said.

I leaped to the bedroom door and tore it open.

CHAPTER 33

Lush Life
or
Skip *au Boudoir*

The four-poster bed lay empty.

Peg was not there.

"You tricked me!" I howled at Skip.

Stout did not stop Skip. He lunged for his black leather coat hanging on a wooden coat rack standing in the corner. My foot lashed out. The coat rack fell to the floor. The coat clunked alongside.

I reached inside the coat and grabbed two gold-plated .45 Marine Corps Commemorative guns. The globe-and-anchor emblem gleamed over brown walnut grips.

"Your tailor sewed gun-pockets into this coat for you," I said. "Remembered you bragging, showing me and waving them. What're you doing with Marine Corps guns anyway?"

"Lady colonel gave them to me. Said that I was the first man to relax her."

"Spare me. Where's Peg?"

"Now, Maxwell, how long we known each other? You like Peg? I can get you six sex beauties better than her with just a phone call. You interested?"

"I'm interested in walking up one side of your dump and down the other."

Skip heaved a great sigh and rolled his eyes. He wore a baby-pink sleeping sack garment with a cord knotted around his waist. It wrapped around his bulk.

"You way different from Joey?" he asked. "Holding my pieces like that? Threatening? Like some thug?"

"I'm different."

"Yeah?" He loosened his voice and let the volume build. "Then just show me how."

"Said Peg was in here."

"Peg. Is that all that you can focus on?"

"What drives your boat? Civil Rights and love for all?"

"Maxwell, what drives me ain't Peg. Kiss that gal, keep your hand on your wallet. Cash is all she wants, Maxwell."

"Flog drinks to drunks all night long, you'd want to escape, too," I said. "She —"

Skip lunged again.

He sprang into the bathroom. I dropped the guns, jumped and reached him around the neck.

"AAARGH!" he gargled.

He twisted free and shoved me back through the bathroom doorway and into the suite. The bathroom door slammed. The lock clicked. Skip was inside the bathroom. I could not get to him.

"You something else, Maxwell," Skip said through the door. "Slickster, my man. Find the fat old man like you did. Knew how much I dig this hotel."

Skip sounded calm, like we were chatting at a country club somewhere.

"But I'm more slick. That's why I told Joey that you'd scam the Ferris Street address from the TV station 32 BJ. We waited for you on Ferris Street, to buy you off. But Joey's hard to control. Doesn't think ahead. Throwing the rock was his idea."

"I owe Joey for that," I said. "And for Peg."

"Did you know this was the biggest hotel in the city?" Skip went on.

BAM! My shoulder hit the bathroom door. It did not budge or buckle.

"Stop trying your distraction on me, Skip! Come out of there!"

The gold .45 guns lay on the floor. I scooped one up and yanked back the slide. The metal racked.

"Know that sound, Skip? Your own gun. Now, open that door before I do something stupid to you in that ridiculous sleep get up. Never saw a grown man wearing anything like that."

"Hate being cold," he said.

"You look like a giant pink Lady Finger pastry."

"With a chocolate center," he said.

"Come out."

"FIRE!" Skip bellowed in his deepest church choir voice. "O Jesus, just look at those flames!"

"Shut up, Skip!"

"BIG FIRE!"

"What you gonna do, Maxwell?" Skip said in his normal tone. "Shoot through the door? Hear those rooms opening up here? Security be here in a New York minute."

"Why d'you always think faster than I do?"

"FIRE!"

"Could just shoot you through the door."

"That makes you a hooligan."

"Or take your guns."

"Makes you a thief."

Outside, doors slammed open.

"They coming for you, Maxwell!" Skip caterwauled. "Guards, firemen, cops, that Internal Affairs lieutenant, the FBI and them hairy radical kids. Oh, yeah, I pay attention. You getting any good by a burglary charge on you here?"

Outside, Gerry's voice clashed against others.

"Security!" Gerry shouted. "No fire here!"

Skip was right, as usual. I remembered the .357 Magnum that Gerry carried illegally and loved to show everyone who cared enough to look.

I slipped out the door and into the hallway.

Gerry's hand snaked under his tweed jacket when he saw me.

"Royster, what the hell?"

"Skip's just having an episode," I said. "Send him the bill. I just quit."

CHAPTER 34

Intelligence
or
Running from a Non-Fire

Henry Street blasted me with cold as I skirted the crowd outside the St. George Hotel.

"LAY NANOON CHOOF HATHA?" a mournful-looking fat man in a topcoat over purple pajamas shouted at his wife as she wept tears. He locked eyes with me. To break his stare, I had to say something New Yorkish.

"What's up, pal?" I said. "You blaming her for the fire that you can't see?"

He gaped.

"Us New Yorkers always give a running commentary on situations around us," I said. "Part of our culture."

The Fire Department's Engine 205 and Ladder 118 trucks roared down the street. Christmas wreaths on the chassis bounced and waved.

When the trucks stopped, firefighters unhitched themselves in that heavy-footed New York style. They had seen everything before. Flaming roofs had collapsed under them and fiery gases poisoned their bodies. But they kept moving on, never showing fear. I envied that.

Two RMP cop cars rolled up behind the fire engines. They looked bored, not likely to leave their warm car until the spring thaw.

Gerry clambered out of the hotel, gold security boss shield swinging on a neck chain. He pointed at me.

"Royster!" he shouted. "Freeze! You're under citizen's arrest!"

"'Freeze,' that's the wrongish kind of word," I said. "Not for tonight."

My feet unfroze enough to carry me away. He might finger me to the cops to save face. Tomorrow morning, he would have to lie to his bosses about letting me inside the hotel or risk losing his job. He would sure know what to do.

"Citizen's arrest off the property and thirty feet away," I groused. "Dream on, Gerry."

The noise faded behind me as I kept looking for Skip's Cadillac.

A man sprawled on a stoop nearby, surrounded by plastic bags. Gray whiskers bloomed over his collar, matching the long hair. He wore a windbreaker, baseball hat and filthy blue jeans.

"Not enough clothing there, partner," I said out loud. "Might freeze to death. How about a shelter, just for tonight?"

He did not stir.

"Let me repeat my question," I said.

"Heard you," he said in a high-class British accent. He sounded educated. Something weird had brought him down low. Maybe it was love. "So, bugger off, will you, mate? Don't need any shelter."

"You might die."

"No!"

"Don't know what that means but you need a shelter."

"Piss off!"

He rolled to his feet, dandling a small axe, nicked and scraped from fights.

"Hold it, partner!" I shouted. "This ain't the way!"

He stepped in. The axe swung.

By then, I was flying away. Feet pounded.

"This, not what I need!" I shouted. "Not tonight. No more gymnastics."

Nobody saw our little street dance. Brooklyn looked like a gray tomb, rimed by frost.

Throwing a look behind me, I cooled it. He was gone.

The cell phone felt cold against my ear as I struggled with my conscience about calling it in.

Finally, civic duty won out over common sense and I punched in 911.

"Police Operator 6029," a shrill Asian woman's voice said. "Where is the emergency?"

Moving my cold mouth, I gave her the stuff about my new friend with the hatchet.

"Don't want him arrested," I said. "Just get him into a shelter. Too cold for anyone to be sleeping out tonight."

"Yeah," the operator said. "Got two deaths already to-night and the shelters are packed."

With that heroic task behind me, I kept slogging through the streets.

Skip was no marathon walker. He would park his prized Cadoo near the hotel. Finding limousine rides by street hailing would be tougher for him than for me. Drivers still felt that some Black men at night might rob them, no matter how well-dressed they were. Racism still poisoned late-night Brooklyn.

A whiff of frying meat caught my nose. It smelled wonderful.

Following the scent, I turned onto Joralemon Street and saw pink neon reading "Diner- Steaks- Chops-Seafood."

"I'll take all three," I said.

Opening the door to the diner felt like entering Heaven's cafeteria.

The lights flickered as I slumped down at the first table near the door.

"Sorry, sir," the squat Latino waiter said. He sported a Zapata moustache going gray and a diamond stud in his ear. "We have trouble, the lights, all night."

"Good news. Couldn't see anything. For a second, thought I was in love."

"Bring you a menu, sir."

Before he did, I remember my head going back against the seat cushion. And I slept.

∾

"I tell you all," Professor Kevin said, looking at us high-school seniors about to graduate and spring into unknown universities. His gold-rimmed glasses waggled over his barbershop quintet style moustache, a darker shade of ochre.

"All about love," Professor Kevin said.

CHAPTER 35

Romance
or
Visions in Winter

In my dream, Professor Kevin breathed deep and looked upwards, grinning at warm blue sky. A calm lake lay behind him, dappled in sunlight.

In my dream, colors exploded. Blue, green, white and ochre burst into sight.

"You can always fall in love," Kevin said. "It's a quickening of your blood, heightened beauty in everyday articles. Age has nothing to do with it. Feel this warm air off the lake caressing our skins this morning. Enjoy the scent of lilacs, fresh young grapes and new-mown grass. Blend these with the wonder of your love everlasting."

Still dreaming, I saw Peg across the crowd of students. Her tanned skin shone darker in the sunlight, under exquisite black brows.

"Who can tell us about love?" Professor Kevin asked.

I took a deep breath and sang out. Somehow, I knew the lyrics of the song. My voice soared and dipped. The song kept flowing. I sang out Peg's name and her beauty.

The students gaped at me.

Then Peg's smile flowered. She looked at me.

"I remember the sweet sleep after making love with you," I said. Maybe I was singing these words, I did not know.

After all, I kept telling myself, this is a dream.

One youngster giggled.

She showed bright red hair, freckles and silver braces on her teeth.

"You can't sing!" she cawed. "Your voice is awful, awful, awful!"

"Really atrocious," a chunky boy wearing a buckskin fringed shirt, bright scarlet pants and white leather boots said. "Shut up, huh?"

They were all around my age of 17. Peg looked like a teenager, too.

"Now, gentlefolk," Professor Kevin said. "This is an open forum, in our Garden Of Love. Anyone can speak up or sing out as they please."

"I sing in private!" a familiar deep voice boomed. "Mutter up her middle mouth!"

Skip appeared behind me, dressed like a pirate with a black eye patch over his left eye and a full grown beard, twisted into wisps around his face. A cocked hat slanted over his head. Wax candles stuck out from the hat.

A cream muslin shirt and stiff canvas pants covered his bulk. He waved a shiny cutlass in the air above him, using a fencer's wrist motion. A leather sling across his chest held four flintlock pistols with chased silver butts. He smoked a dark cheroot.

That killed my song.

"Skip!" I blurted. "Why are you a pirate?"

"Cause you keep calling me a courtroom pirate, baby!" he thundered.

"Who is this?" Professor Kevin yelped.

"Pirate lover," Skip said.

A tall sailing sloop sailed on the lake behind him. As we watched, it got closer.

Moving with the speed that always surprised everyone, Skip lunged for Peg.

The sky turned dark.

He gripped Peg around her narrow waist, using the cheroot to light the candles in his hat. Now he looked like a demon, face lit by candles.

"Run for your lives!" Kevin said.

The students fled.

"This be prime spring meat!" Skip chortled.

"This doesn't make sense," I said.

"Course not," Peg said. "This is a dream."

"Oh," I said. "Then that makes it all right."

The sloop came in closer to the wooden dock on the shore.

"Come," Skip hissed in Peg's ear. He pulled her towards the dock.

"Leave her alone!" I hollered. "I'm falling for her!"

"Then keep your hand on your wallet, Maxwell."

"Butt out," Peg said, looking at me. "I like Black guys with cash."

Skip bore her to the dock's end. The sloop bobbed there.

I started running towards them. It felt lopsided. Skip hauled her over the sloop's gunwale and dropped her onto the mossy deck.

Other pirates, cutlasses and daggers and pistols, jammed into their belts, ogled Peg.

"Cast off!" Skip shouted. "Got what we need right here!"

I ran harder.

The pirates used pikes to push away from the dock.

The sloop drifted six feet away.

I got closer.

The sloop went farther.

I reached the end of the dock and LEAPED! for the sloop's rail.

I missed it.

Chill waters slapped my face. I could feel my shoes and my clothes dragging me down. The water was dark below the surface.

Thrashing, I came back up in time to see Peg kissing Skip. Her hand roved across the sling of pistols and under his blouse.

"Peg, don't!" I shouted, spitting out water. "You don't know how he is!"

Swimming like a madman, I reached the sloop. A rope from the sloop trailed in the water. I seized the line and pulled myself closer to the sloop. My hands turned to chalk. They crumbled into dust. The sloop sailed away from me. Peg and Skip laughed at me from the deck.

Someone shook my shoulder.

The dream ended.

∾

My eyes opened.

In half-light, the same Latino waiter was touching my shoulder. The restaurant was dark.

"Sir, you gotta leave now," he said. "Power died. We closing here."

CHAPTER 36

Cold Pavements, Again
or
Tahiti Beckons

The waiter stayed off to my side, ready to bolt.

"I was dreaming," I said.

"Is okay," he said in his Spanish accent. "No sweat, man. You all right? Don't wanna get too cold, right?"

"The years keep adding up, partner. This might be Our Hero's last all-nighter. And you're closing?"

"Got to, boss. Can't run the kitchen safe without no power."

"Aw, raspberries! Cold out there, partner."

"Very cold."

"Detective genius Gerry McQueen says that there's always one more question to ask, one more door to knock on. So, look at my phone here. Have you seen this guy in here tonight?"

"This Black guy?"

He squinted at one of Skip's newspaper photos on my phone. As my contact lenses cleared from my sleep, I saw that the waiter was older at second glance. Hair silvered towards the crown of his head and his neck skin wattled and flowed over his shirt collar. Maybe tonight was aging him fast. Perhaps it was aging me, too.

"Might have been driving a big Cadillac," I said. My words tried to slow down. If the question sounded hurried, the answer might come back thoughtless and too fast. Usually, time helped the researcher. Tonight was the exception.

"You a cop?"

"Do I look young enough to be a cop? Thanks. No, no cop."

"Private detective, maybe? Pay for me to tell you?"

"No, I'm not a PI, either."

"Got a private investigator, Mr. Siegesk, come in here, eat a big steak dinner every Sunday. Say he make a lot of money. Why don't you do?"

"Because private eyes now are sometimes sneak thieves for the rich. They whore for landlords to throw out tenants and jack up the rent. When CEO's sex-harass secretaries, PI's protect the CEOs against lawsuits by threatening the secretary. Companies sell defective cars. When someone dies in an accident, the car company hires private eyes to 'investigate' any claims. Some investigate by asking the super how many liquor bottles come out of the complainant's apartment."

"They can do that, boss?"

"Private eyes can do anything. And some of them do. If the state lifts their license, they just work under someone else's ticket."

"Sorry about the electricity, boss."

"You didn't blow the fuses yourself," I said. "See you in Hawaii."

Outside, Brooklyn Heights looked just as stark as before.

The air cut sharper.

Wood smoke scent announced that Yuppies were going natural tonight. The brownstones looked like they were lined in frost, down to the chill black metal window gates.

"Doing fine, Royster," I muttered. "Lost your only handcuffs and half of your edged weapon. Great detective, on ice."

A siren blared its importance. Another car honked, not agreeing.

"Hawaii," I grunted. "Maybe Tahiti."

No limousines rolled on these streets.

My fingers pressed the cell phone apps for more car services in the area.

"Voicemails," I muttered. "Watch me turn into a crabby old man. All I get are voicemails."

Another three blocks and my feet numbed again.

I turned the corner and stopped.

Skip's Cadillac lay parked at the curb.

CHAPTER 37

Mechanical Skill
or
Cadillac Genius

Skip's Cadillac stared back at me.

The tony street boasted brownstones and SUVs. Brooklynites on this block had plenty of the ready.

To protect those SUV's, they also had bright lights brimming from their front stoops. Some local tycoons might be awake now, not tied to tomorrow's time-card of a Saturday. They could look out their French windows and see suspicious blue-collar me skulking near their motors.

"Our Hero must move now with vigor," I said.

My teeth chattered from cold.

My phone iced my ear as I called my limousine driver, Orville.

"Unknown Number, whachoo putting down?" Orville said, by way of greeting.

"Action that maybe you can't pick up," I said. "No names here, please. This is the feckless jasper that you just dropped off in Brooklyn Heights."

"Palaver, Unknown Number."

"Need a biped who knows Cadillacs. Especially the older sharkfin models. I'll pay top dollar."

"You got any god dam idea how cold it is out here tonight?"

"Where d'you think I am right now?" I asked. "In a Turkish bath? Montague Terrace and Remsen Street. I'll be waiting. And freezing."

"Can't do it, Unknown."

"'A man's reach should exceed his grasp,'" I quoted. "John Dryden, I think. So, try."

"You're dreaming."

"Montague Terrace and Remsen."

The call ended. So did my energy.

"Back into a frigid doorway for our hero," I said.

Following my words, I molded myself into the building line where no nervous brownstoners could espy me.

Chill minutes dragged me.

My head felt heavy as I arranged myself onto a brownstone stoop and tried leaning backwards. That strained my neck. So I leaned forward and shut my eyes again.

These brownstoners knew that they lived a half hour walk from the Red Hook Housing Project, awash in dope deals and murder. Anyone could prowl here and rob or steal. So they would watch out for anyone hanging out on their street during this chill.

Some Brooklyn types would exit their homes and address the problem themselves with a golf club or Louisville Slugger baseball bat. But these brownstoners would summon the forces of law to chat with me. That might derail my scheme.

Orville's limousine slid down the street and I stepped out to flag him down.

Orville stepped out with his passenger in front seat.

The passenger was a thin bent youngster with a crooked nose under a knot of black curls. He sucked on a Marlboro, maybe to warm his throat.

"I'm Cumberbatch," he said in a voice that grated through his nose. "Know Caddies. Whaddya need?"

"Pop the trunk so the driver doesn't notice," I said. "Then I get inside, close the trunk and get out when I gotta."

"Show me the car," Cumberbatch said. He scratched his crotch.

"I'm staying with my ride," Orville said. "Between you two. I don't know nothing."

Cumberbatch looked over Skip's Cadillac.

"Where does this jamoke still find shark fin Caddies? Museums? They're fricking classics, bro."

"Got a dealer," I said.

"Bad news, Chief. This model, I gotta bust the trunk lock to open her. You get in, we close it okay, nobody can see it. But it's gotta be locked. Not held shut, one hand, like I figured. You're in, pal. And gotta be good with tools, to get out again. You okay with tools?"

"I can spell the word," I said.

"Then, forget it. You could kick off in there. Then, I go for manslaughter. NG, baby, no good. On parole now. Not worth it to me."

Logic went out the window then. I wanted Peg.

"I don't care much about me," I said. "But I think you're shucking me. Shucking and jiving. Don't think that you can get inside that Caddy, anyway."

"Yeah?"

He slumped across the street, melted into the shadows and metal sounds snicked in the chill air.

He came back and showed me a dirty gloved palm. Three ignition locks were in the glove, along with a wallet and wristwatch.

"Just did those three rides," he rasped. "Don't tell me what I can't do. Now, you got me outta warm bed, ace. Short notice, too. A grand to get you into the Caddy and out again."

"You just hit three innocents to prove a point?" I asked. That was the ex-cop in me talking. "Gonna mess up their day."

"Tough," he said.

"Five hundred."

"You get what you pay for, pal. I gotta take care, Orville. Referral fee, like. Cuts into mine."

"Five, Cumberbatch."

"Chisel me and I get mad. See you're a softy. Maybe I take off every car on this block, you make me get my gonads all twisted. How you like that?"

Nothing moved.

"Don't like that," he said. "See it in your face. Softy, yeah."

"Six hundred. Or else, I take off now."

"Six, okay."

"Let's Orville find us an ATM," I said. "Quick. Don't want to lose the Caddy now."

CHAPTER 38

Pricing Service
or
Here's My Knife

Orville drove me onto Jay Street and next to a drab superette. A New York Fire Department ambulance stopped across the street. Two Emergency Medical Techs shambled out and leaned over a white-bearded man lying on the sidewalk.

"What gives, over there?" I asked Orville.

"What look like?" Cumberbatch said.

"Citizen over there looks graveyard dead," I said. "Shame."

"So, what?" Cumberbatch sneered. "Shouldn't be fartin' around, lyin' down, cold like this. Pro'ly drunk on Sneaky Pete wine. Serve his butt right."

"Hate to have you for a landlord, Cumberbatch," I said.

"Yeah, bro'," Orville said. "Homeless ain't no crime. Guy could be your daddy. Old enough."

"Not MY daddy."

"Got a family somewhere," I said. "If he'd gone inside somewhere, he'd be alive by spring thaw."

Trying to shake off the dread feeling, I went inside the superette. It smelled of cigarette smoke and cats.

"ATM?" I asked two unshaven men watching a soccer game someplace warm and tropical.

"Corner, next to candy," the shorter one grunted in a Middle Eastern accent.

"Thanks. Where's this game?"

"Our home. Jordan."

"Tonight I'm jealous of everyone living anywhere warm," I said.

"You visit. Beautiful."

"Not tonight," I said. "Bit busy."

Cold made my hand shake with my VISA card at the ATM. But the technology held and cactus colored bills spurted out.

"Orville and Cumberbatch may try a rip-off," I muttered to myself. "Even for just six hundred clams, I could be an endangered species."

At the cash register, I watched the two Jordanians and their soccer game.

"Who's playing?" I asked, to speak with honest types, for a change.

"Jordan play Russia. Think who we want win?"

"Can't imagine," I said. "Do you gentlemen sell any large knives for cooking?"

"Knives?"

"Yessir. Giving a big dinner party for friends and gotta carve up a roast. Need a big knife."

"No, my friend. Nothing. Try Duane Reade."

The younger one kept watching the soccer game.

"Maybe, someday, we Jordan people play Israel in soccer," he said. "Hope they don't cheat."

The scissors-dagger chilled my left wrist and I tapped it, trying to calm my nerves. Nobody was selling big knives anywhere near here tonight. Everything I had rested on my scissors-dagger.

As they watched the game, I folded the cash and jammed it down into my left sock. This was no time for a rip-off. This was the morning to get Peg and have her in my bed by noon.

My nerves kept clanging against my head. Skip might be lowering his girth into the Cadillac right now and spiraling away. This was my last chance for Peg. Back in Orville's limousine, the scissors-dagger felt ready to go.

Being around hustlers was corrupting me. Orville just drove us three merry innocents back to the Cadillac and we got out. Nobody tried a rip-off. Not yet.

"Don't look," Cumberbatch said. "No witnesses."

Orville and I turned away from him.

THWONK!

Skip's Cadillac trunk swung open.

"Hey," Cumberbatch said. "Somebody forgot to close their trunk. Maybe we should stay here until the owner comes back to lock it."

"Good idea," I said, facing away from him. "Even without looking, I can tell you was a Boy Scout."

"Trunk's open," Cumberbatch said. In his strong hand, he held a tan pointed piece of animal horn about eight inches long. Something like cord or maybe deer sinew was wrapped around the butt.

"Native American horn knife," I said. My voice shook again. "I saw them at trade shows."

"Indian gut-ripper," he said. "I ain't politically correct. Pay up time."

"Aw, Cumberbatch," Orville said. "Make everyone paranoid like this."

"Not at all," I said. My voice still wavered. "Here's the cash. Six hundred round iron men. You earned it. That horn knife won't ring metal detectors, right?"

"Why I bought it. Nothing stops me. Looking at this trunk latch here, you got a problem."

"Pray tell."

"This year model, I can close it okay, you inside. But I gotta lock it or else it flies open at your first bump. You're locked in. Need some tools, some luck and a lotta time."

"Tools?"

"No place open now for tools like we need."

"Loan me your horn knife."

"Dream on. Cost me a bundle. And you may get killed doing this. Then, where's my knife?"

"How melancholy. I got a scissors blade. I'll show it to you. Okay? Don't get tense. See it?"

"That blade won't work. You're nuts. Freeze in there. Might die."

"Lock me in," I said.

I scrunched inside the trunk.

Cumberbatch closed the trunk cover over me.

"Hold it!" I shouted.

He froze. The cover stopped.

"Okay," I gulped. "Just panicked there. Now, close it."

He did.

It locked.

I was trapped.

CHAPTER 39

Close In
or
Life in a Trunk

Trying to get warm, I snuggled back into the fetal position. It did not work.

Outside my trunk cover, Orville and Cumberbatch moved and spoke and I could hear them on the silent street.

"He might not make it," Orville said. "Why's he doin this?"

"Some don't care," Cumberbatch said.

"Nice epitaph," I said aloud.

They did not hear me.

Cumberbatch snorted and laughed.

These might be the last men that I ever heard and I was doing this for a woman. Think that one over.

Car doors opened and shut. Nobody wanted to linger in this chill.

Jack London stories about gold miners freezing to death in the Yukon came back to me.

"Frostbite at zero degrees can come in 45 minutes, with a wind of ten miles per hour," I said aloud. Nobody could hear me and the sound of my own voice comforted me. I did not know why. This trunk was teaching me things.

"It was eighteen degrees, the last I heard," I said. "And wind no more than five degrees. So I might last a while longer."

"The experts say you feel sick and hungry when the body starts to freeze. Stay tuned to this station."

Then I started to drift somewhere towards sleep.

❧

"They damn fools, giving us this case!" Skip raged. "Call this adjuster boss, Germante, nobody knows where the blue-ribbon hell he is! Maybe he gone in the crazy house!"

"Don't care for the case much?" I asked.

"Boy named Thau goes up to a Jewish orthodox summer camp in White Lake, New York. Up in the piney mother-kissing woods! Once Thau got to camp, he got chickenpox. Nobody know how. They tried isolating him, sent his young tail back to the city. But the camp was already infected. Twenty-four l'il darlings caught the pox. Last one was a kid named Reese. Like Pee-Wee Reese, huh? That a Jewish name?"

"No such thing as a Jewish name, Skip."

"So Reese's daddy be a bloodsucking lawyer. Files the papers himself, no charge since he a lawyer, free ride, and sues the camp. Wants to know who infected these crumb-catchers first. Camp resisted. Then, their lawyers said, give up Thau's name. They did. So, Thau wants a defense, asks us to go to White Lake and investigate the claim."

"How?"

"You figure it out. Go up there and do SOMETHING. Interview mallard ducks, for all I care. Find Pocahontas, take off her buckskins, see if she got chickenpox anywhere. Me, I go north of Yonkers, those upstate rednecks want to shoot me with their grandpappy's deer rifles, to prevent integration and us darkies stealing they blonde virgins."

"Remember, I don't have wheels," I said. That made me feel ten years old.

"Go see Honest John Di Laurenti at his car lot. He got something special for you."

Honest John Di Laurenti sure did. He loaned me a red PT Cruiser and pointed me north towards White Lake. Leaving the Thruway, the road got lonely. Cottony snow blanketed everything. Green trees stood like mint sticks against the white. No houses showed anywhere. That worried me. As a Playpen city boy, I needed to see some neon or a torn newspaper.

The Something Special power steering died and I skidded off a mountain road, down a ten- foot incline and into a deep snow bank. The door trapped me. I could not move to free myself.

I kept struggling. It was early February and freezing cold.

"Window's down," I said. "Hear a car on the road and I'll hit the horn. They'll hear it, stop and find me."

No cars passed me.

The cold tightened around me. I struggled but could not move.

Something scrunched on the snow near me. My head turned and I locked eyes with a young white-tailed deer four feet away. He or she regarded me with curiosity.

"Hey, there," I said to the white- tail deer. "Who was it, first gave chickenpox to young Mister Thau?"

The deer just kept looking at me.

"I'm investigating, Skip!" I shouted at the top of my lungs. "I'm asking everybody!"

"Hey!" a man shouted in a country twang. "Don't move there!"

BAM! BAM!

Shots hit the car around me. A side window exploded.

The deer leaped away and vanished.

A burly hunter-type in a red plaid jacket, holding a scoped rifle, came down from the road. His buddies, rifles still smoking, trailed behind him.

"What you doing here, in that car, there?" he asked.

"Deer hunting," I said. "New system."

"Another city wise guy. Been tracking that deer all morn-ing. Now, we lost her, thanks to you."

"And your hawk-eyed marksmen over there," I said. "Don't forget them."

He sighed. Grey stubble covered his pale wide face, un-der a low blond hair-line. His jaw worked chewing something. Maybe it was deer meat jerky.

"Guess we gotta get you outta there," he said.

"Would be nice," I said. "I never been this cold in my life."

CHAPTER 40

Skipping Sex
or
The Wild Man

Inside Skip's trunk, the cold kept digging into me.

Drifting in and out of sleep, I could not ease into sleep.

Banging on the trunk might get someone's attention. In Brooklyn Heights here, they would purr into their jeweled cell phones to 911 and get me rescued and kill my plan graveyard dead.

So, that was out.

❧

Our jet banked over the beach at Rincon, Puerto Rico.

"We meeting the client's team at the Hermosillo Airport," Skip said. "He needs a team of bodyguards cause everyone looking rich gets kidnapped here sooner or later. He gonna show us the jungle and beach property that he owns. Supposed to be the best in Puerto Rico. Look at that blue damn water down there, Maxwell. We in Paradise, son!"

"Seems like you're right," I said. I scanned the world outside the clear Lexan polycarbonate window.

Our jet crested over pale blue waters, with cream wave-tips breaking far below us. I could see the curve of the shore-

– 137 –

line, pinked against the sunset. Surfers tore tiny reams in the water, zigzagging and tumbling.

As we banked, the sun came through the window, warming me more in my only dark suit. It felt generous, after the wintry blasts back in Manhattan.

"Two weeks down here, meeting with our client and his local counsel and doctors," Skip said. "All on him paying the freight. Even if this case don't go nowhere."

"The case will go somewhere," I said. "It already brought us here."

❧

Later, I slipped into sleep.

My head banged the trunk and I woke up.

"This is hell," I whispered. "Trunk's too small. No air. I'll smother. Hell. What the nuns warned us about."

My body shriveled against the cold.

Sleep came and went.

Something slammed.

That woke me.

The car rocked.

Maybe Skip was getting inside here.

The car moved.

My mouth opened so hard that my jaws ached. I wanted to shout for joy.

"After I get through thrashing this fine young lady," Skip's baritone boomed from the front seat to the trunk. I could hear every word in his courtroom delivery voice. He must be talking on his hands-free cell phone as he drove. Skip always wheeled at high speed, controlling the Cadillac like a pro racer.

"Got up, went to the little boys' room and put some cold wa-wa on Willie and the Twins. After she scraped them somehow. And Willie and the Twins, they ain't had cold water on them in thirty years. Nossir."

Hearing Skip's voice was like diving into a bathtub of hot coffee and whiskey, blended. It comforted me that much.

Somehow, I was going to untangle myself from this messy night without end and stand beside Peg.

"Fat old me crawls back out, the bedroom, tryinna be quiet," Skip rolled on from the driver's seat. It was hard to believe how his voice carried, all the way back to my frozen ears in the trunk.

"So, she wakes up, re-arranges her face to greet the world, asks me 'Walter, when are we getting married?'

"Now, you know they ain't nobody on Jesus' earth, calls me 'Walter.' I be 'Skip' to the whole wide Black-and-White-and Mulatto world. 'Skip.' Just a tired old man, skipping round the truth. And now, the old man is tired! Just a old tired man, standing by the messy bed."

"Makes me ask her, 'Now, darling, sharp and foxy as you are, don't you know the difference between getting married and foolin' around?' So, she says, 'Walter, just what we doing?' I say 'We just foolin around. Yeah, thass all. Foolin' around."

His voice brought back the happy, laughing times, serving as a handmaiden to the law and getting stiffed by the clients sometimes.

Perhaps my scheme tonight would hurt him. Maybe I would back out to protect him. Maybe I did not know what I would do.

CHAPTER 41

Chow
or
Dining *al Fresco*

We kept traveling.

Skip bounced and skidded taking corners.

Some shaded corners of the city still had ice. The pale winter sun had not melted those spots.

An expert like Skip could not control the big Cadillac when he hit the ice patches. The Cadillac slewed around.

Sliding like a hog on ice, my head banged against the trunk's wall again and again.

"This keeps up, I won't be able to remember my own name," I whispered. "Have to wake up and look in my wallet, see who I am."

"But," I said, continuing the monologue, "it distracts me from the damn Klondike cold."

We kept moving through the night.

There was no telling where we were. Everything sounded the same cold dead same.

Stories of kidnap victims went through my head. In 1933, Machine Gun Kelly had kidnapped and blindfolded Charley Urschel, taking him almost 200 miles deep into the heart of Texas. Urschel, a wealthy oil wildcatter turned millionaire had the kind of precise mind that recalled the smallest detail. He counted minutes to himself and remembered when the road changed from asphalt to dirt, whenever a train whistle blew and what time an airplane passed overhead.

In country Texas, 1933, planes were rare. His memory helped the FBI catch Machine Gun Kelly and the kidnap gang.

But I was no genius oil tycoon like Charley Urschel. I fell asleep.

Skip stopped.

My head hurt.

I realized that the wall had hit me again. Or, I had hit the wall.

"Either way," I grumbled. "Something gotta change."

Skip's Cadillac had stopped. This was my wakeup call.

The front door opened and Skip's weight leaving made the car lurch.

"HAUGH!" he said, getting out.

Doing anything made him grunt like that.

The car door slammed.

This could be my only chance. He might be meeting Peg, still held by Joey. Or Joey, held by Peg. Sex was funny that way. Someone might die laughing.

My fingers tried working the scissors-dagger free from the band on the left wrist. The fingers felt brittle.

I found the trunk latch and worked the tip of the blade into it, back and forth.

Nothing worked. The lock did not give. I tried jiggling the tip gently. Somehow, it reminded me of experimenting while making love, back and forth, rocking on hips and play-ing. My thoughts were starting to swirl around mad. Tonight there was too much cutting up wild and not enough sleep.

My wrist rotated to every angle. It was no good. This lock was standing firm against me and my toy weapon.

Maybe I had cheated myself by not lugging a gun around, like most other hooligans did. Guns repelled me and I always wanted to be different and just look where it got me tonight.

For some reason, I slid the scissors-dagger back under my wristband. It was doing me no good.

My head tilted back and I slept again.

At least, I think I did.

The front door opened, the car shifted under The Great Man's weight and the door slammed again.

An aroma came backwards to me in the trunk and I knew that there was no secret rendezvous with Peg and Joey, not yet, and I knew why Skip had stopped, gotten out and come back.

The aroma was White Castle hamburgers with onions, relish and catsup, extra-spicy, the way that Skip liked it, and crisscross jumbo cheese fries. The oily smell filled the Cadillac and its trunk. Skip could not live without this combination and he ate it once eight times in a week when we had worked together, according to my count.

"Ain't no stereotype, bout us Black folks liking cheap fast food," Skip had told me that week. "I mean, it's a real stereotype."

"Skip," I had said. "You know what they say about folks who stereotype others?"

"What do THEY say?" Skip asked, eyes bulging out.

"They say that they're all the same," I had said.

That was why he had stopped, at the White Castle on Utica Avenue and Remsen, open all night, never closed, and only had take-out through a bulletproof window on the side-walk. My gut wanted him to toss me a few burgers to gnaw on myself but he still thought that he was alone in his Cadillac, gorging himself on animal fats and salts.

After a bit, we started moving again.

CHAPTER 42

Subpoena Toss
or
Is It Legal?

We kept bumping. The roads got worse.

Ocean smell wafted into the trunk. Maybe we were in Rockaway Beach.

My fingers crisped through my pockets and came up with the maybe-fake subpoena. Maybe it was real, maybe it was fake. But, aside from my scissors-dagger, it was all I had.

Skip stopped. The door opened, weight shifted again and the door slammed.

"That's it," I hissed. "FINIE. The end. Our Hero's getting outta this trunk."

Pressing the scissors-dagger point into the trunk lock again, I tried jiggling the mechanism. Locksmiths had told me to do this with a sticky lock.

So far, it was not working for me.

The scissors-dagger twisted between my frozen fingers.

"No deal here, sports fans," I said aloud, to keep my spirits up.

Outside, a door shut. Voices came near me.

"None of this makes sense," a woman said.

It was Peg's voice.

That thrilled me. The soft city accent, the babyish lisp and her slow delivery spurred me to jab the scissors-dagger harder into the lock.

The lock held.

"Now, dahlin'," Skip said nearby. "You just leave all that to the old man. He knows the game, knows about how the cow ate the cabbage."

Skip was pouring on the oil for the witness. For years, I had seen him do it and it always worked. Angry wits would curl up in his lap and see him once again as Big Daddy Fix.

"You're pulling me in and out of hotels like I'm an escort," Peg said. "But you're gonna make a lot of cash from me. Like better treatment."

"All for your protection, my sweet," Skip wheezed. "This just the first night, things unsettled —"

My blade spun around more.

Another man grunted but I could not hear what he said. Maybe it was Joey.

"So far, I haven't seen anything," Peg said. "Watch me walk away from you, right now."

Was she bluffing?

I dug harder. BAP!

The lock gave.

Panting, I surged up. The trunk rose. The scissors-dagger dropped.

I came with the trunk, squinting against the sunlight.

Peg gaped at me. Her pink mouth opened. She still wore the same black suede and wool coat. Joey and Skip started for me.

I spun away from them. This had to be quick.

My hand snatched the crumpled-up ball of subpoena paper from my side pocket and winged it at Peg. For proper service, the paper had to touch her. She saw it and dodged sideways. My ball was going to miss her. She could run free.

The Cadillac stopped her. She banged into the car's front panel on the passenger side. She flung out a hand against the car.

The subpoena paper ball hit her hand.

"Legal contact" I shouted. "Subpoena! You're served!"

"No way!" Joey shouted.

My head swiveled around. We were standing in a motel parking lot. The Coney Island boardwalk loomed behind him, in gray daylight.

Skip bent and yanked the pearl-handled derringer from his ankle holster. It pointed at me.

"Joey, you're on camera!" I hollered. "Video right there!"

Joey pivoted, looking for a camera. There was none. I was bluffing.

I tried getting past him. His forearm slammed into my face. I saw black.

"Stop it!" Peg shouted.

His fist exploded everything. Sagging back, I gut-punched him. His leather jacket protected him. My punch had nothing behind it. There was nobody watching, no help coming. Just a Christmas fist fight between buddies.

"Gonna break you up, old man!" Joey shouted. "Put you on a walker!"

I dodged two jabs and twisted away. Joey looked about forty. I was twenty-three years older.

My shoe scraped his shin. He grunted and belted me a wild combo, like a street fighter.

He got behind me. His arm went across my throat. Tobacco smell and hair oil mixed. He cut off my wind.

I elbowed backwards. He held on. I was blacking out fast. My ears roared. I sank downwards. I was going to die right here in this parking lot.

CHAPTER 43

Showdown
or
The Law Speaks

Someone hit us.

We three sprawled.

I smelled perfume. Peg slammed into us again. Joey's arm got loose. I elbowed him in the gut.

"Joey, kill him, you screw my money!" Peg shouted. "Stop it!"

Skip aimed the derringer at us and shot red flame. His arm went up. Smoke showed. Maybe he shot at Joey. Maybe at me.

A car alarm screamed nearby.

I head-butted Joey. He gasped.

Peg grabbed his arm. With his other hand, he jabbed her hard on the face. She dropped.

He choked me again. I tried bending backwards. Something stabbed me in my side pocket. I reached inside the pocket. It was my scissors-dagger. It had fallen into the pocket when I came out of the trunk.

I was blacking out. I reached up with the scissors-dagger and raked it across his strangle arm. I put all my weight and strength into it. The blade did not go through leather.

Things swam in my eyes. Throat pain turned me wild. I stabbed backwards at his face.

"Awww!" he screamed.

I jabbed again. His arm loosened. I kept stabbing.

His arm dropped. I reached back, grabbed his collar and slammed him into the Cadillac's grille. My scissors-dagger fell. I slammed him again, aiming his head into the bumper. He curled up and dropped to the asphalt. My foot went back and kicked him in the head. I could not stop.

I looked to Skip. He held Peg by the waist and dragged her to the Cadillac. Joey's punch had dazed her. Her head rolled loose.

"Got another bullet here, Maxwell!" Skip said. He waved the derringer.

"Use it!" I said. I leaned back against the car, measured and kicked upwards to Skip's free arm. My foot hit his elbow. He dropped the derringer and Peg.

"Sweet," I panted. "Just like in the movies."

Behind us, faces showed in the motel windows.

"Cops!" I screeched. "Lotsa cops. BEAUCOUP cops! A plethora!"

"That ain't gonna help, Maxwell," Skip said. "All we need is some common sense and mother wit."

The derringer in my hand was blued steel, with white pearl grips. It reminded me of a dark chocolate cake with cream icing.

The adrenaline dump hit me.

My head dipped.

An NYPD car whipped into the parking lot. Two cops, one an Asian woman with dyed blonde hair, the other a pudgy Black guy with a handlebar moustache, bellied out.

"Royster, off The Job," I said. "Call your Duty Captain and Lt. Hundshamer of IAB and Evers of the FBI."

"That all?" the woman said.

"City Comptroller, too, if he isn't too busy," I said.

"You call, champ!"

"Cover yourself," I said. "Get bosses here. This is a hair-ball."

"No FBI," the man said. "I ain't studying no mother FBI."

"Famous But Incompetent," I said. "I'll call."

Four more cop cars screamed here, brimming with worried sergeants. They looked more worried when TV vans showed and camera crews started filming everything.

A Coney Island Hospital ambulance slammed to a stop. A blonde woman paramedic glanced at us, getting out.

"Check muscle-face over there," I said, pointing at Joey. "He's knocked out."

She grimaced, bent down and took his vitals. Her face tightened.

"Knocked way, way out," she said in a New England accent. "Dead. Probably heart attack."

I felt sick. My hand pitched the blooded scissors-dagger far away. Nobody saw it.

"Don't nobody go nowhere," the woman cop said, scanning me. "You, especially. With all that blood, your face."

My hand found something wet on my cheek. It was likely Joey's blood. I had no cuts.

The Duty Captain, a rail-thin sad Latino bloodhound with lines down his face, surveyed the scene. Skip refused to talk with him. Hundshamer arrived with lights and sirens going. He clutched a manila envelope and glared at me, up close.

A dark blue van marked "Kings County District Attorney's Office" in orange pulled up. Another character, Black, bearded, hefty and business-suited, joined us.

He spoke with the Duty Captain and then moved in on me.

"Subpoena service," I said. "All legal. Get her to show you the paper. He attacked me."

"Bull," Hundshamer said. "Book him for manslaughter, Counselor."

"Skip over there shot this gun at me," I said. "Here, take it."

"Got a permit," Skip said. "And I was tryinna save Maxwell from Joey. Ask him."

"Who, Joey?"

A blue SUV, red light bleeding, bounced into the lot. Evers and a white-haired Senator type, maybe her boss, got out, flashed their gold badges and came through the police ranks.

"Federal Civil Rights case," Evers said. "Our jurisdiction."

"Don't you ever stop?" Hundshamer said. "You, girlie. Peg? What did you see happen with Yates and Rajarr the cop?"

"Not here," Peg said. "I'm not giving it away."

"You better," he said. "Or else, I hit you with a Material Witness order and you go into civil jail. Right, Counsel?"

"Maybe," the ADA said. "If she proves uncooperative."

"She don't gotta talk now!" Skip wailed. "I'm her lawyer!"

"Not if I get you disbarred," I said.

"Uncooperative?" Hundshamer said. "Like maybe perjury? In a homicide case?"

"What perjury?" Peg asked.

"That's enough," Skip said. "Don't say anything."

Peg looked at her. Her jade eyes blinked. Now, they showed fear.

This could be my hook into Peg.

"Peg, lawyer, schmawyer," I said. "You perjure yourself, you go to jail. Not your lawyer."

"Huh?"

"Wanna protect you from this mess," I said. "I get Skip disbarred for shooting at me, you got no lawyer –"

"Get her another in a New York minute," Skip said.

"Peg, you're scared now," I said. "Never saw you like this before. Why?"

"Tell you why," Hundshamer said. He ripped the Manila envelope open and fanned out black-and-white photos.

The photos showed Krio Yates inside the garage and on top of Rajarr the cop. Yates and Rajarr both had their hands gripping a black gun. They were fighting over it.

Further up the garage ramp, another photo showed Peg's high heels. She was beyond the curve of the garage ramp. There was no way that Peg could have seen the struggle. In this photo, Rajarr was firing his gun into Yates' body.

"We've got continuous video film from the garage video cameras," Hundshamer snapped. Now, he was scaring me. "This shows that Yates WAS trying for Rajarr's gun. Picture proof."

"Maybe Yates was defending himself against police brutality," Skip said.

"Try that one with no witnesses," I said. "Yates suffered diabetes, acted drunk, got irrational and jumped Rajarr. Peg, you saw nothing, right?"

"I saw it!"

"Camera says you didn't. Shoes are too far away. The ramp twists to the left, remember? Curve blocked your vision. You just want money, right?"

"We catch you perjuring on this," Hundshamer said, "you gotta leave New York. Everyone'll know your face. Records say you're a barmaid. Nobody'll hire you. Get pickets front of their bar. Give it up, kid."

"I saw nothing!" she said. "Nothing, no way. That's what I got."

Everyone seemed to exhale. I know I did.

"Royster killed this mutt lying down over here," Hundshamer said. "He goes down for that."

My body iced over again.

This was turning to a nightmare.

"Let's review that," the ADA said.

Skip waddled out towards the TV vans, holding out his arms like a country preacher.

"Lemme tell you about another po-lice cover-up!" he roared. "Right before our eyes! They threaten our only witness with perjury and scare her into recanting. Nobody never put her under oath. Ain't no perjury here!"

"No eyewitness, either," I said.

"Royster walks on this death, Lieutenant," the ADA said.

"What?" Hundshamer shouted.

"Subpoena looks valid to me," the ADA said. "Captain Mora here agrees. Royster served it legally and this thug attacked him. Can't have that. Royster used force that was reasonable and necessary, to protect himself. The heart attack was not his fault."

My knees buckled.

Peg's hand caught me. She gripped me and leaned me against the Cadillac.

"My tough guy savior," she said. "You need guidance, old man."

"Not guidance," I said. "Just you."

"Me? Looks like I'll be a barmaid forever now."

"Not with me, you won't. I'll help you climb this Manhattan ladder."

"And what'll we have?" she asked. "Just sex, right?"

"Sex, to start with, sure," I said. "But, then that changes to love. Right now, at Christmas."

Special thanks once again to...

To Detective-Investigators Mark Baldessare and Gerry McQueen and all the other cops and federal agents who taught me so much about hunting our real-life serial killers.

To the *Spy, the Movie* team – Jim MacPherson, Alex Klymko, Charles Messina and all the rest of the gang for a grand adventure in screenwriting.

To Nad Wolinska for her always inventive cover illustrations.

To Richard Amari for his equally inventive cover design.

To my screenwriting partner, Lynwood Shiva Sawyer, for his support and encouragement over the years.

To my talented editor, Michael Simpson.

If you enjoyed reading *Love Finds Max Royster at Christmas* or *Kissing in the Slush after Sixty,* you'll definitely like Frank Hickey's other Max Royster novels:

Max Wisecracks Hollywood
or
Foxtrotting for Justice

I, Max Royster, cannot run fifty yards or see my own feet under a beer belly.

Pushing sixty-four years old, I struggle to rebuild, after the New York cops fired me for depression and hijacked my pension.

Like everything else sliding around loose, I wind up in Hollywood, California.

By chance, I see a female Black LAPD cop grapple with a homeless woman, an ex-Blaxploitation film actress who 40-years ago turned Civil Rights radical.

The homeless woman dies.

Sidewalk Angelenos heave rocks and bottles in protest.

Los Angeles screams. Cops retreat and haul me to the station.

An ambitious Deputy District Attorney and the hard-charging FBI play witness tug-of-war over my fast-aging body. Everyone wants to jail me as a material witness for trial.

To stay clear, I go underground with a cryptic Hollywood beauty and learn much on the floor of her apartment. The media turns up the heat. The G-men freeze my cash.

All that I have left are my wits and the cash in my blue jeans.

When the Whistle Blows, Everyone Goes

Federal agents jail me for murder. That's me, Max Royster. Aging. Fat. Broke. And innocent. How do I clear myself from inside my cell? Nobody believes me. A hate group tries to rape and kill me. But Mother Royster always said to keep smiling no matter what. So to chase away the jailhouse blues, I organize a hipster group and swing dances among the inmates.

A Manhattan tycoon frets about his beautiful daughter.

She is cavorting somewhere near Palm Springs, California.

He pays me, Max Royster, to find her.

This simple job turns into a hairball.

She leads me astray.

Someone kills her boyfriend.

The U.S. Park Rangers blame me for it and lock me up in a federal prison.

Me being me, I try to stay cheery by organizing swing dances between male inmates.

An inmate hate group tries to rape and kill me.

Other inmates protect me for kicks.

Some enjoy the dances. Anything beats prison routine.

The warden and the correction officers suspect me of spying on them for the FBI.

Things look grim for our hero.

Can I swing-dance and laugh my way out of lock-down to find the real killer among the Beautiful People in Palm Springs?

Everyone wants to see what happens next.

You will, too.

Softening Flatbush

I, Max Royster, fat, broke, divorced, thrown off the NYPD for mental illness. Now in Flatbush, Brooklyn, I find new love, new murder and new career. Can I keep my love? Crack the case? Can I inspire and change private security? And maybe regain my NYPD shield?

Flatbush, Brooklyn, a neighborhood that used to be the borough's jewel.

Sixty years later, street crime plagues the area.

My love, Cooper, and her friends want to clean up the neighborhood and improve Flatbush's image. That way, they can 'flip' their homes and triple their profits

I join a security agency, thinking I can transform the guards from unhappy minimum wage-earners to passionate, hardworking crime fighters.

If I succeed and make Flatbush safe for Cooper and her friends, we will buy a home there and enjoy a happy marriage.

My new employees and I fight to take back the Flatbush streets. I give them better training, uniforms and weapons. The guards buff their new badges with pride.

My boyhood friends, out-of-work actresses, barflies and story-tellers, join us in our quest.

But some guards refuse to let go of old vices. Others turn vigilante and bully innocents.

Curbing their zeal, I try to teach them to uphold civil rights as I hunt the suspect in the comedian's murder.

Then, under cover of night, good and evil clash at the Lefferts Historic House. Facing disgrace and prison, I must decide what matters most in life to me.

Come walk with me on that razor edge between brutality and staying alive as Cooper and I, my Flippers and my guards give everything to try Softening Flatbush.

Can Showbizzers Crush Crime?

Can I, Max Royster, fired from the NYPD for mental disease, on crutches, train a ragtag group of performers, my Showbizzers, to use their skills and bodies to stop a genius crime lord in the High Desert town of Basta, California?

Freezing, grieving my lost shield, I hobble aboard an Amtrak train. America passes by outside my window.

When we reach the California desert, my spirits rise. Hope for a new life makes me exit in the small sandy town of Basta.

The sun and beauty cheer me. But the town suffers from crime. A thug mugs me, taking my cash and ID.

That turns me sad again.

A group that I dub "My Showbizzers" – out-of-work dancers, actresses, dog trainers and writers – rescue me. They remind me of my live-for-the-moment cronies back in Manhattan, "The Playpen Irregulars." Thrilled by their energy, I fall in love with Koy, a beautiful Asian dog-handler.

Some Basta deputies duck work or bully innocents. Their sloppiness angers and frustrates me, and their laziness helps a local criminal genius, Crostwaite, rob a bank.

My Showbizzers have many skills. Maybe they could use those talents and creativity to fight crime. They might do better than some lazy deputies.

Nobody else believes in my idea. Locals mock me. The sheriff and the FBI block me. But I force myself to push my idea forward, while my Showbizzers must fight their own bias against government and rules.

But when Crostwaite starts killing, I train my Showbizzers. They go undercover. Their beautiful bodies use sex as a weapon. Koy trains dogs to burgle homes and seize evidence.

To avenge his childhood of horrors, Crostwaite vows to destroy Basta.

Frightened but passionate, without guns, power or respect, my Showbizzers and I risk everything to stop Crostwaite.

Our deadly showdown will answer the question once and for all: *Can Showbizzers Crush Crime?*

Brownstone Kidnap Crackup

When Max witnesses a debutante's kidnapping, he becomes the FBI's prime suspect. Or is he actually their salvation?

It's Christmas in Manhattan.

A blizzard whips the city.

The Beautiful People, in the elite Upper East Side, celebrate in their brownstones.

Until a kidnapper seizes a beautiful young debutante.

Max Royster, fired from the NYPD for mental illness, fights the kidnapper but loses.

The kidnapper flees. Stripped of gun, shield and power, Max has only his wits to save the victim.

The FBI treats Max like a suspect and tramples roughshod on his rights.

During this long sleepless night, an unknown FBI agent cracks up. Over the radio, he quotes J. Edgar Hoover and plants false clues.

To solve the case, Max must smash through the facade and mysteries of millionaires in their snug brownstones.

Exotic women tempt him to give up.

The blizzard worsens.

As the winds howl and snowdrifts deepen, Max risks his life and his freedom in a desperate bid to save the victim.

Once again, Max Royster is back on the street in *Brownstone Kidnap Crackup*.

Funny Bunny Hunts the Horn Bug

To catch a sex killer targeting Upper East Side beauties, misfit NYPD cop Max Royster goes undercover…as an NYPD cop!

The Upper East Side of Manhattan is one of the richest neighborhoods in the world.

But Max Royster, a maverick, outspoken and erudite NYPD foot cop, who grew up working-class in this tony area, calls it "the Playpen." Money protects the bluebloods in this area like the bars on an infant's playpen.

Late one night, patrolling wealthy brownstones, he sees a burglar attacking a rich actress. Max chases him. They fight but the burglar escapes.

The burglar is a sexual predator, known in cop-speak as a "Horn Bug".

For losing the suspect, Max's captain deems Max "a Funny Bunny," too unstable for police work. He strips Max of his gun and badge, then orders Max into Bellevue Hospital for observation and maybe for the rest of his life.

Without any tools or support, Max has ten days to stop this Horn Bug.

Max Royster's hunt for a sadistic serial killer takes a startling turn when he realizes that not all predators are born alike.

One autumn night, someone strangles a teenage boy jogging in Central Park.

In Brooklyn, street cop Max Royster risks his life to disarm a madwoman with a knife without harming her. Nevertheless, her lawyer charges Max with brutality. The Department decides to punish Max.

Max's protector is Sgt. Lipkin, an expert detective working the Central Park murder. Lipkin knows that a killer like this seeks a new sexual thrill, a "Gypsy Twist," with each new murder. The dead boy is the son of one of the wealthy elite of the Upper East Side. Max is the only cop in the city from that world, and on scholarship years before, Max had even graduated from the dead boy's school.

Lipkin summons Max for the assistance that only Max can provide.

Max probes the tony school and neighborhood, ignoring bosses who, out of jealousy, try to block his progress.

A beautiful, free-spirited reporter, Diana, woos Max to try and make him reveal insights about the case. Denying him nothing, she lures Max onward.

The killer seizes another school-boy who was playing soccer in the park and drags him to death with a car.

Wealthy New Yorkers scream that someone is butchering their sons. The city rocks.

One night, muggers attack Sgt. and Max, who freezes on the trigger. The muggers cripple Lipkin.

The Department moves to fire Max.

But the dead boy's tycoon father hires Max to track down the killer. Max and Diana live below the radar in the New Orleans and San Francisco underworlds, hunting the killer until a shocking conclusion reveals the killer's true identity.